AF268695

A Collection of Mythic Tales

Hades Had a Son

A Zimbell House Anthology

Hades Had a Son

A Collection of Mythic Tales

A Zimbell House Anthology

ZIMBELL HOUSE
PUBLISHING
UNION LAKE, MICHIGAN

This book is a work of fiction. Any references to historical events, real people, or real locales are used fictitiously. All characters appearing in this work are the product of the individual author's imagination, and any resemblance to actual persons, living or dead is entirely coincidental.

All rights reserved, including the right of reproduction in whole or in part in any form. No part of this publication may be reproduced, distributed, or transmitted in any form or by any means, including photocopying, recording, or other electronic or mechanical methods, without the written permission of the publisher.

For permission requests, write to the publisher:
"Attention: Permissions Coordinator"
Zimbell House Publishing
PO Box 1172
Union Lake, Michigan 48387
mail to: info@zimbellhousepublishing.com

© 2018 Zimbell House Publishing

Published in the United States by Zimbell House Publishing
http://www.ZimbellHousePublishing.com
All Rights Reserved

Trade Paper ISBN: 978-1-947210-34.9
Kindle ISBN: 978-1-947210-35-6
Digital ISBN: 978-1-947210-36-3
Library of Congress Control Number: 2018902379

First Edition: April/2018
10 9 8 7 6 5 4 3 2 1

Acknowledgments

Zimbell House Publishing would like to thank all those that contributed to this anthology. We chose to showcase five new voices that best represented our vision for this work.

We would also like to thank our Zimbell House team for all their hard work and dedication to these projects.

Contents

Not Your Hero   **1**

M. L. Allison

Restorer of Life   **21**

Linda M. Crate

Second Chances   **37**

Noah Daniels

Spring Is So Annoying   **123**

Michelle M. Monagin

The Best Laid Plans   **139**

Christina Lengyel

Contributors

A Note from the Publisher

Other Anthologies from Zimbell House

Coming Soon from Zimbell House

Not Your Hero

M. L. Allison

Baruch stared across the river of Styx at the souls waiting for passage. Some of the older ones waved half heatedly before turning back to their conversations. He ignored them, letting his thoughts run past and around him. "Why do you think he wants to see me now?"

Charon hummed, keeping the rowing even, almost gliding over the water. "Don't know. Maybe he has some time and would like to get to know you. You are his son, after all."

Baruch's face scrunched up. "He's had over twenty-one centuries, and he didn't show the slightest inclination to get to know me even when I was standing right in front of him. I don't think that's it."

Charon clucked his tongue, and his image flickered to a skeleton-esque figure in a flash of temper that Baruch had grown used to. The spirit passengers still tried to huddle on the other side of the boat away from him. "He's not going to punish you. You've caused enough trouble with that cursed spirit that you would've been called down far sooner if that was the case. Maybe he wants to acknowledge you, give you a job now that he thinks you're old enough. Why are you so worried?"

"I've heard stories up there of deities playing with their children's lives like it's some game to them, heard of them using them and their deeds as some trophies to elevate their position. I don't want to be that. If he doesn't want to have anything to do with me, I can handle that, but I couldn't stand him pretending to care and having to force a smile like everything's okay." Baruch turned to look at the immortal that had raised him since he was a little baby, born in the underworld from a mother whose soul had slowly faded away.

He docked the boat on the other side of the river and motioned for the other spirits to leave the boat, glancing back to the gentle looking man he seemed to prefer. "Few know the mind of your father. Give him a chance, and he may yet prove himself."

Baruch snorted. "That's why I'm going, isn't it?"

He climbed out of the boat after the spirits and watched as Charon started rowing to the other shore. It felt like he was being left in some shady city to make his way. Even if he knew he could run back to Charon, there was something about this that made him almost feel abandoned.

"Baruch! You've grown so much!" The shrill cry jolted him back as his step-mother launched herself at him. He staggered back a step, but she was pulling away just as quickly, pinching his cheek. "I see you're no longer tearing up your father's kingdom with that little-cursed spirit. Cerbeces has missed you terribly. Oh, by the way, your father sent me to show you the shortcut, so you don't have to deal with all the melancholy spirits."

He bit back the urge to tell her that Hades wasn't his real father, wasn't a father in anything more than name. Instead, he forced a smile. "Really? I miss him too. I just don't have as much time now that I'm helping row the boat back and forth. How's the orchard doing? In winter bloom yet?"

She grinned, taking his arm and guiding him along the bank away from the other spirits heading for judgment. "Like the silver sketch of a tree in moonlight, and the flowers are just as gorgeous. Pity you don't have the talent of handling life like I do. I could use a hand in the garden."

"I was under the impression you weren't my mother." Baruch silently cursed himself the moment it was out. He wished Akon, the cursed spirit, was here to make the running commentary. Baruch knew it was better to keep quiet.

Luckily, Persephone just laughed it off with a sound like a tinkling bell. "Oh, you aren't. Born down here after I killed your mother because apparently there was no way you weren't coming out. I was so angry that I almost tried striking you down again, but I'm glad I didn't. You proved yourself. An immortal!"

She sighed almost dreamily, clasping her hands, and Baruch tried to take a discreet step away from her, but she wrapped an arm around his shoulders, pulling him closer. Her eyes gleamed in a way that left Baruch feeling like the spirits on Charon's boat when he flashed his true form as she whispered in his ear, "You've always been more mine than your fathers'."

Anger rushed through him, and he roughly shook her off. "I'm Charon's."

She laughed again. "Of course, you are, dear. So loyal. I can't wait to show you to Hera. She'll be so jealous. That Jason boy doesn't come close to you."

Baruch's guard was instantly up. He wasn't much involved in the running of the Underworld, but he knew that other than Persephone and Thanos the other deities didn't have anything to do with this realm. It was almost jarring to be reminded how deities viewed the immortals, especially since he didn't have their vast control over an element. He was only an immortal, and it had been almost a pride since Charon was also an immortal. Here with Persephone, it was more like a weakness he was ashamed of, and he hated himself for feeling that way.

"Ah! Here we are." Persephone turned to face a nearly invisible door that didn't seem to go anywhere, with what seemed like pride.

Baruch looked at the door doubtfully. "This is the shortcut?"

"Well, it doesn't look like much, but that's part of the point. The Underworld keeps changing and growing; we needed something that would just stay put, to … collapse the distance. It was a mortal doing. She was very talented. Your father's thinking about hiring her to do more projects for as long as her little mortal life will allow. Pity you can't extend their lives." She shook her head and opened the door, revealing an orchard dressed in a cold silver.

He stepped through the door, a little more curious to see how it stacked up against what he remembered from when he was a child. It seemed smaller, but he supposed it might have something to do with Persephone having come back down not that long ago and him being bigger than he had been last time.

The door closed with an odd metallic whirling sound. He turned. Persephone was eying him like he was a wolf in the midst of a hunt. He took a step back and swallowed. She wouldn't be affected by a handful of spirits that might come to his aid and down here he couldn't exactly raise corpses. He briefly wondered if it was possible for Akon to come down while he was with a host and if his presence could curse a deity.

"Beautiful, isn't it?" She asked, stepping closer. "Maybe after you're done with your father, you can come back here, and I can give you a more complete tour. I've got one that's growing a child; it should bloom before I leave."

Baruch didn't want to know. He shook his head. "You're not taking me to him?"

She gave him an indecipherable look. "Oh, no. I still have to attend to my plants. He's through the door and all the way down the corridor. It shouldn't be too hard to find."

She left him to wander among her trees, lightly touching their trunks. She wouldn't be a very attentive mother, but she'd probably be a little more involved and caring then Hades was. After all, she'd been more involved in his life than his own genetic donors. Even if Charon rolled his eyes every time Baruch came home with one of her bandaging jobs, she wouldn't be a terrible mother if she had someone a little more grounded to help take care of the child.

He shook his head free of the straying thoughts and looked around for another door. Hades Palace was on the other side of the orchard and peeking out from behind a couple distant branches was a round wooden door that clashed with the obsidian look of the palace. He'd never been in the palace before so he couldn't say if the door had always been like that or if it was newly installed like the shortcut door. It didn't really matter; he still made his way over to it.

The door creaked opened like any other door, and Baruch felt a little disappointed. He stepped into the corridor, letting the door fall closed behind him. The inside matched better with the looming Obsidian look of the outside. The corridor walls were just as black and glassy, with tapestries hanging from the ceiling detailing the history of the Underworld in mostly black with a lot of orange and red. It felt comfortable, familiar and yet foreign.

Baruch slipped into the room at the end of the corridor and immediately saw that Hades wasn't alone. His whole body tensed, and he had the brief thought of just flipping Hades off and leaving, but it wasn't too hard to imagine the deity taking out his frustrations on Charon. He could never betray his real father like that. So, he closed the door behind him and acted like he didn't want to tear the place down with his bare hands.

"Ah, here's my son now," Hades announced from his ebony carved throne, bringing the other deities gaze to Baruch. Hades probably didn't even know his name.

"You requested my presence?" Baruch gritted out, holding his hands behind his back so tightly it almost hurt in the vague achy way he couldn't focus on.

Hades smiled at him, and maybe it was sincere, but Baruch wasn't looking that deep, didn't want to look that deep. "Baruch, my son. My family has talked me into choosing a hero like so many of them have. I told them you were the best one for the job."

His blood ran hot, and all that effort to keep himself civil was gone. "No. No, you don't get to ask me. No, I won't be your hero. No, I won't be your perfect little son. And no, you don't get a say in my life. So, take all your little deities buddies and burn in Tartarus. Because you aren't my father!"

He stormed back out, not paying attention to the deities' reaction. His heart pounded and his blood heated with pure rage at the audacity of Hades. He'd left Baruch to be raised by Charon who'd help birth him in his boat, hadn't even had the nerve to talk to him in his twenty-one centuries, and now he expected Baruch to be willing to just leave his real father behind for something as transparent and chaining as fame.

"Breathe. Breathe." The wispy spirits murmured the same word like a breeze, and he jolted to find himself in the Apsophel fields. The dead were flowing around him, and he felt his breath leave him in a sudden panic. He was seven centuries and lost. He'd never been this far from Charon's boat before, and all these spirits were surrounding him, whispering the word he was crying out.

He snapped himself back. Charon had taught him how to navigate the entirety of the Underworld and even Tartarus if he got lost that far from the river. He sighed and looked down at his hands, realizing that he could've sentenced Charon to some retribution for his refusal. There was blood shining in little crescents on his wrist from where his fingernails had dug in. Charon wouldn't say anything about them, but he'd have a look on his face that would make Baruch feel worse.

"Home. Home."

"Yeah, yeah. I'm going," Baruch muttered, feeling a little better as one of the spirits brushed a wispy hand against the side of his face. The dead here had a tendency of picking his mood and blending in with it. They'd been the first sign of his powers.

"To the West?" A stray voice whispered amongst the crowd, and it sounded so much better than having to face Charon and tell him what happened. Tell him how wrong he'd been about Hades.

***

"Let me get this straight. The guy who never bothered trying to accept his child-rearing duties suddenly wants to claim you ... so he can show you off to all his deity friends as a slave—oh, sorry, I mean 'hero,'" Rajiya, one of the immortals of the west, checked herself. She tossed back a shot with an elegant roll of her eyes. "Your father is a complete ass."

"Charon's a wonderful guy. Why would you say that? I mean, sure he tries to make excuses for Hades, but he's a wonderful father," Baruch teased.

Rajiya's eyes sparkled with laughter as she struggled to swallow her drink. They were at their favorite bar that catered to immortals in the area or those just visiting. The other two had yet to show up, but Baruch didn't worry too much. They both had other business to attend to as well.

"What are you two up to?" Avion asked as he took a seat beside them a moment later.

"Where's Akon?" Baruch asked.

Avion's eyes gleamed as if he knew what Baruch was up to. "Stuck with the youngest girl in the Capri family. She's got fire in her from the little glimpse I caught. Sounds like they bicker a lot, but who doesn't he bicker with? You should visit them when you get a chance."

Baruch nodded as he watched Avion pull some chocolate and dried fruit out of his bag. Rajiya reached around Baruch to try to steal one of the chocolates, but Avion caught her hand without even looking. She made a noise in the back of her throat as she leaned back.

"Our dear Baruch has been approached to become a hero of the Underworld. Naturally, he turned it down with as much venom as he could muster," she filled Avion in.

"I'll remember this next time you need a friendly hand in dealing with a couple minor deities you got into a brawl with."

Avion laughed.

"Hey, do you often visit the Capri hosting Akon?" Rajiya broke in. "That must be interesting, visiting a bunch of girls from different generations and aging so much slower than them. I can just see you perched on the same fence with a scowl while the neighbors gossip. 'Isn't that the same boy dating that dated that poor soul who died fifty years back? Why the Capri's must've enraged some deity.'" She turned her voice into a shaky imitation of an old woman.

Baruch gave a half smile and turned back to Avion. "What do you think I should do about the whole situation?"

Avion shrugged. "You made your decision, and you meant it. I think you should stand by it. Definitely tell Charon what happened though. You should've gone to him first. He's probably worried sick."

Baruch silently held out his wrist. He felt Avion's warm hands turn it over and gently touched the marks. Rajiya leaned over to try to get a look, and Baruch bolted to his feet and out of the bar into the streets. Avion was right. He should go back to Charon, tell him what happened, but he didn't want to admit what happened and see the disappointment on his face.

A cry jolted him out of his thoughts, and he looked up to see a car barreling toward a six-year-old girl who was standing frozen in the street. Something about her looked vaguely familiar, and he didn't think, just launched himself across the street and grabbed the girl, pulling her out of the way a second before the car zoomed past. She trembled against him, and he could hear faint little sobs against his chest.

At that moment, he was never more glad that immortals were a little faster and stronger than the average mortal. He smoothed the girl's dark hair aside and brought himself to her level. There was a slight air of death around her that he hadn't noticed before. *A demigod of Hades.* That was why she'd looked familiar. He knew he'd had half-siblings, but they'd all been mortal, and he'd never actively looked for them.

"Hey!" Baruch looked over his shoulder to see Avion making his way over to him with Rajiya in tow. "What happened?"

"He saved me," the girl said.

Avion shared a glance with Baruch before crouching beside her. "Where are your parents?"

She sniffled a little. "I don't got any. Cause I, I can tell ..." She looked around and dropped her voice to a whisper. "I can tell when someone's gonna die."

Baruch smiled and lowered his voice as well. "Yeah? I can make the dead rise again and control them."

Her eyes widened in awe, and then she giggled. Avion looked impressed. He probably thought that because Baruch spent so much time with the dead, he wouldn't be so good with kids. Well, he'd met some of the younger souls that had the misfortune of dying too young, and he'd done fine keeping them calm even when Charon lost his cool and showed his true form.

"Why don't you come with me, and I'll give you a safe place to stay, okay?" Avion offered, holding out his hand for her to take.

She looked at him for a long moment then looked back up at Baruch. "Do you think someone's going to die? I can feel death nearby."

Baruch reached for the pocket watch he kept in his pocket that Thanos gave him. The god of death was almost like an uncle to him. He had more contact with Baruch than Hades had. In fact, the guy had brought Baruch along on a couple of his jobs and had gifted him a watch that could affect mortality. It was the only one of its kind.

"My name's Katty, by the way," She announced, before taking Avion's hand, glancing at Baruch as Avion lead her away.

He pulled his hand away from the watch and stood up. Rajiya came up toward him, watching Katty leaving with Avion. "What was that about?"

"I don't know, but I'm going to check on her. After I talk with Charon."

It took the better part of the day to convince Charon that he needed to take the night off to check on his half-sister and that he was convinced she was in fact, his half-sister. In the end, Charon only seemed to let him go because he thought time away from the Underworld could help the situation. Baruch wasn't sure he was right, but he wasn't going to argue.

The room was dark when he arrived at Avion's sanctuary for the gifted mortals, budding immortals, or the ones who had a longer lifespan than the average mortal for some reason. Avion was collapsed in one of the corners with one of the younger ones he was caring for snuggled in his arms.

There was a silver light hanging around Katty who was thrashing in bed and sounded like she was struggling to breathe. He pulled out the watch and held it over her. She had less than an hour left on her mortal time; this wasn't natural. Anger and indignation rose in him. She was a daughter of Hades; part of the Underworld ran in her veins. This wasn't right.

He moved the time needle closer to her seventies. She wasn't going to die this young, and from what he could tell, she moved in mortal years, not even the immortal centuries that counted as years in their books. There was more resistance than there should've been. Baruch's stomach sank. He wouldn't. Not his own child. The needle stuck at twenty-two.

"Harsh. Who all is capable of interfering with the watch's power?" a familiar voice asked from behind him.

Baruch snapped the watch shut and looked over his shoulder at his best friend, his partner in crime, Akon might as well have the last name of the family he's cursed with, Capri. There was something almost more reassuring than Charon about having him at his back, feeling the misty, barely-there feeling of his hand as it touched his shoulder.

"The Lord of the Underworld and Death himself are the only ones that can fight the watch like this. You feel the aura around her?"

Akon tilted his head, moving around Baruch. His hand shifted around Baruch's shoulder as he studied the girl. "It's not just about her dying is it?"

"I think she's my half-sister. I've had a few. Mortal like her. He tried to make me into one of those 'heroes' the other deities make their ... favored children into. I told him to go to Tartarus."

Akon's silver light flickered, and he winced. "I'm sorry. My bond with little Picta Capri is still developing. I apparently can't leave for too long. You should go give your 'father' a piece of your mind, and maybe remind him he already has one child he doesn't pay attention too, he doesn't need more." Then he completely faded out.

Baruch sighed and turned to wake Avion and tell him what happened before heading back home. Akon was brash, despite being a half immortal year older than him, but Baruch had to admit that he wanted, needed, to face Hades, needed to make him know that he wouldn't stand for this, wouldn't stand for his—for his FATHER—to kill off his own children like this.

Fire simmered in his chest like he'd just downed a couple of immortal drinks as he strode out of Avion's little sanctuary for the mostly outcasted magical. Katty would be safe there, while he confronted the deity.

Baruch marched through Persephone's garden and orchard. One of the trees had an odd couple of growing bulges that bent the branches toward the ground. Something about that unsettled him. He supposed a child was growing in it for Persephone. He pushed aside the unease to finish storming into Hades palace. That was Persephone's problem, anyway. He wasn't really related to those growing buds anyway.

The hallway seemed darker and less familiar and comforting than when he'd been here earlier. It seemed more like a pit to Tartarus that part of the Underworld as he neared Hade's throne room.

The other deities were gone now. Only Hades was sitting on his throne. Something dark and unfamiliar lurked in his eyes as he watched Baruch defiantly approach him.

"She's my half-sister, isn't she? And you tried to kill her." Baruch glared at him with all his might.

Hades tilted his head. "She's mortal. She'd die eventually, but I see you managed to change her fate anyway."

"You have no right to be anyone's father if you would so callously kill one of them. I'd rather be Poseidon's son than yours!"

Hades face darkened dangerously, but Baruch continued on. "You should've had the good sense to at least leave us alone if you're not going to care for us. We can do just fine without you."

Blue fire erupted on the back of Hades throne like elaborate decoration. An unsettled feeling clawed it's way into Baruch's gut, warning him, and in that brief moment, he thought about turning back, going to the safety of Charon and pretending that this encounter hadn't happened. Then Katty struggling for breath came to his mind, and the impulse vanished like a morning fog. He wasn't going to let a deity treat everyone they saw as beneath them. Someone had to stand up for the mortal children deities drug through their own version of Tartarus, for the kids they killed off like they didn't matter.

"What did you say?" Hades growled, hands tightening on the arms of his throne.

Baruch narrowed his eyes. "I said you're no father of mine, and you don't deserve to be a father to any of us."

The room erupted in blue fire, and the earth trembled only the way a true lord of the Underworld could cause. Hades was off of his throne and wrenching Baruch off his feet by the collar of his shirt. "You insolent boy! I offer to make you a hero to raise you above your lowly roots. I allow you control of part of my domain, access to the watch of mortality, and you dare throw it back in my face! Let us see how far you make it living like any other immortal." He tore the watch from Baruch's side belt and held it in his hand, with a dark glint in his eyes, he looked at Baruch. "A watch like this can't ever be truly destroyed, but I can make it so that neither you nor any other immortal may touch it."

Baruch felt his chest clenched as Hades threw the watch and it rippled through the walls. Hades didn't even look at him as he threw Baruch against another wall, power oversurging his circuits. Baruch's head hit the wall, and everything went dark.

***

"You did this?" Charon's voice was surprisingly neutral as he faced his lord with the son he'd raised, unconscious in the corner.

"He needed to be taught a lesson. Take him … and make sure he never comes back here again. This is no longer his home. He wants to be part of the uprising immortals, then he can live like them," Hades said in a calm, soft tone, before striding out of the room.

Charon paused before gathering his unconscious boy in his arms. He didn't seem to be hurt too bad other than a nasty bump on his head and a dark bruise by his collar. Baruch let out a little moan and tried to curl into Charon. Charon's heart clenched in his chest, feeling like he was losing his son for reasons out of his control.

Baruch stirred, feeling like his head had developed another heartbeat. He groaned and rolled over, not daring to open his eyes. A presence moved in front of him before a cool hand gently touched his forehead, and he flinched. The hand retracted.

"Charon dropped you off," Avion's familiar voice told him barely above a whisper. "He said Hades banished you from the Underworld. You're to live with us."

He didn't open his eyes, didn't move. His world felt like it was crashing in. Hades had taken away his real father away. He was alone except for the immortals he'd bonded with. The spirits that had chatted with him, the immortal that had raised him, were far from his reach, and the watch of mortality was lost to him forever. His world was gone now. He felt tears burn down his cheeks and curled in on himself.

Restorer of Life

Linda M. Crate

You may have heard of Macaria, Melinoe, and Zagreus. Those were my father's favorites. I was just a forgotten son. My name was Alessandro, and unlike my siblings who worked for father in the Underworld for some purpose, even if it were only to give mortals nightmares, I was the flower bearer.

My grandmother, Demeter, adored me because unlike my mother and my other siblings, I did not stray far from her. I think she wanted to believe I was her son, and so I indulged her because I never really had a mother.

Persephone rejected me as Hades did when they realized that I wasn't interested in staying in the Underworld with them. With so much darkness and despair, I could not endure the lost souls that wept for not having made it to Elysium. It wasn't that my father was unfair to them, but he also wasn't always the kindest. He was passive, a watcher of souls, but he never commented on his judgment.

My mother, I thought, on the other hand, would understand. She had been dragged from her flowers down to the Underworld by my father, and when my grandmother tried to retrieve her daughter, my grandfather, Zeus, insisted that there was nothing he could do to help.

Which was a lie, of course, I'm certain he could have done something, but perhaps that would start a war between the gods, and they would've all taken sides because that's how catty and shallow most of them are.

Demeter had taught me all I could possibly want to know of flowers—all their names, all their purposes, and even how to listen to them. Most people don't know this, but flowers, like trees, can talk. They just choose not to talk to most people.

They are gentle creatures who can feel pain and misery just as any mortal could, but I found they were generally kinder.

Love, I knew, was appreciation and not ownership of a person or any living creature. Or even any inanimate object. This was something I learned whilst listening to my grandmother's tale of woe about her daughter leaving her.

My mother, I was told, would know the significance of the pomegranate. She did it simply to spite my grandmother.

Considering the controlling and obsessive nature of my grandmother, I could understand. However, I never said this as I didn't wish to wound her. She had already lost her daughter and relationships with some of her grandchildren. Those who only preferred the Underworld or doing the bidding of it ignored her.

But I thought that death and life were intertwined. The death of one thing could bring about the life of another.

I admired the flowers that were killed in the winter and then came along each and every spring. Sometimes they would come back in different shades, and that was always interesting. It was as if they were changing their clothes as one is accustomed to doing.

My favorite season was spring with all her life and many splendid flowers.

It was then my mother came from the Underworld to visit my grandmother. Though, she didn't always stay until winter came as she used to when she was a girl. I tried to explain to my grandmother that she had duties as a guardian of the Underworld and children besides, but my grandmother insisted that one should always make time for their family.

I didn't disagree, but I didn't think this was a comfortable relationship for either my mother or my grandmother. My grandmother would speak of my mother like an old friend she couldn't see often enough, and my mother would complain to me whilst she was here of how my grandmother was like the insect that wouldn't stop drawing her blood.

I thought, perhaps, if my mother talked to her mother about it they could sort issues out, but my mother refused to do so.

She would act as if everything were all right, but turn around and complain to me of my grandmother. Almost as if she forgot how she refused me for leaving the Underworld. She used to say how she missed me and would try to convince me to go with her when she left grandmother, but I couldn't break my grandmother's heart like that.

I think my loyalty and devotion to the mother she left behind both hurt and vexed her. She cursed me out once because of it.

My mother insisted that I was hers and not her mother's and why would I want to live here, anyway?! Didn't I tire of flowers?

The answer was that I simply didn't. I loved blossoms. They were full of hope, promise, and dreams.

My sister was the weaver of nightmares, but I was the guardian of dreams. Sometimes I sent dreams that drove away her nightmares, which only seemed to cause further rifts between myself and my parents as they couldn't see why I would hurt Melinoe that way.

I didn't actively seek to, but sometimes I was glad when I was able to free a dreamer from her. She was sometimes cruel, vile, and sinister to people who didn't deserve to suffer in all the ways she put them through.

I knew that sometimes one must suffer before they could know true joy, but I hated how she toyed with humans as if they were puppets on her string and she controlled all the moves. It made me quite ill, to be honest.

Like all my siblings, I had powers. I could restore life where death had fallen, but I didn't often intervene because my father had a quota to fill each month and he warned me point blank not to intrude upon his business.

It was funny how he treated death as a business when he had no business making it so. Death happened to all things and all peoples, but everyone should get the chance to live. Sometimes it's why I brought children and animals back to life, even an old woman's favorite flower once, for she wept so long and hard that I knew she needed her friend.

I was also a guardian of dreams and their dreamers. In addition to those two powers, I could also kill things that had life still in them. I think that was my father's power in me, but I didn't use it.

I made sure to never use it. I wanted him to see that I did not enjoy death, and I could not see how he could take away the lives of people and feel only apathy for them.

Sometimes he would give them an opportunity to rouse their loved ones from beyond the grave, but then he would add some stipulation that they couldn't possibly endure due to curiosity or longing. A game he knew that he would win, and he would insist that he had given them a fair chance.

Perhaps, he did think he was fair, but it seemed rather unfair to me.

Few knew of me, and even fewer sought me out. If they knew the name of Alessandro, then they would have been able to spare themselves some trouble. They probably would have given themselves a better chance at finding their loved ones again.

Sometimes I planted my name on the tongues of mortals so they could be saved. My grandmother said that was sneaky, but she always smirked when she said it. I think she took great pride in that I rebelled so mightily against my parents.

I wasn't trying to further alienate myself from them or my siblings, in all honesty. I was just trying to do the right thing for mankind.

One day my grandmother left the garden we tended, and a young mortal woman found it by accident. I was supposed to drive them out whenever they came, and mostly I did.

However, this one intrigued me. She was tall and willowy with thick dark brown hair that fell past her waist. Her eyes were blue-green like the ocean, and she wore a dress that was bedecked with the design of many tiny flowers. I saw her speak kindly and gently to my grandmother's flowers as if they were friends. She wore a flower crown atop her head.

I couldn't help but smile.

I could feel the power and pleasantry of both her soul and her dreams. She wasn't a bad person in any sense of the word.

After watching her for a few moments, I recovered myself. I walked over to where she stood. "Excuse me, young maiden, but you have stumbled upon a garden of Demeter."

"A garden of Demeter, then who are you?" she asked.

"Her grandson, Alessandro."

"Alessandro?! You appeared to my brother in a dream. You saved his life, you know," she remarked.

She hugged me, which was a completely foreign action to me. I knew humans sometimes hugged one another, and sometimes my grandmother hugged me. But this was the first time a human hugged me.

Her olive skin was warm as the softest, most gentle rays of sunshine and she smelled of lilacs and vanilla.

"I'm glad," I smiled. "But you should know I am the son of Hades."

"Why are you here then?"

"My parents rejected me because I choose to guard dreamers and because of my ability to rouse the dead. I can restore life to those things that have been taken. I have to be careful, though, for my father would be inflamed should I intrude upon his business."

"His business?"

"He treats death as a business. Has a quota of souls to make per year. I'm only allowed to save a certain amount of people. It's hard for me. I hate to see any creature or person suffer."

The young woman regarded me with soft eyes. "Alessandro, I'm sorry your family is the way it is," she said, sincerely. "My name is Anabel. Maybe one day we'll meet again?" she asked. She hitched her skirts and left my grandmother's garden.

"Yes, I'd like that," I called after her.

My grandmother spoke to me that afternoon, but I found myself distracted. I kept daydreaming of Anabel. She was a beautiful soul that saw past the appearance of things and looked straight into their souls, and she was one of those rare humans that could speak to flowers and trees.

For even the flowers were speaking to my grandmother of her.

"Did you not drive her from the garden?"

"I did. I was just taken aback by her beauty."

My grandmother blinked. "So not even you are impervious to the thoughts of love?" she asked.

"Of course not, why would you say that? Even the god of the Underworld saw to take himself a wife."

"That's true, and you are his polar opposite. I didn't think this day would come or perhaps I wished it wouldn't," my grandmother sighed. "You love her, don't you?"

"I've only just met her, grandmother, but if we did wed, would we still be welcome here? She's one of those mortals who can speak to flowers and trees," I informed her.

"Yes, I suppose I'll allow for that. The flowers do speak kindly of her."

Anabel came day after day to the garden. My grandmother watched her with the flowers for several months before making her presence known.

Annabel and I were wed the following spring, which was a mistake, looking back upon it, but I thought nothing of it at the time.

My mother was there to witness the union, of course, and she was most displeased.

She insisted that she was just another woman that had come to take her son from her.

My mother and I fought heavily the entire time she was here, and my grandmother fought her also. But my mother caused rifts with her tongue where she ought not to have and burdened us all with her hatred and her jealousy.

I wasn't sorry when she left. Nor was Anabel.

Anabel had been miserable the entire time my mother had been here. She had cried so many tears that the flowers were even angry at my mother.

Anabel became pregnant that summer. I remember the joy I felt to know that we would have our own child.

My grandmother was elated, too, for I found that she really loved Anabel. My wife was like the daughter she never got to see or so it seemed. All was well for a time.

Anabel would sing to the flowers, and they would sway and dance in the music of her voice.

Little did I know how very spiteful my mother was, and what she would take from me.

For on the day that Anabel delivered our child, this was the day she died. Childbirth had taken away from me, the only sunshine in my life I had ever known outside of the flowers.

The only woman I had ever loved, the only woman that had ever caught my attention in my grandmother's garden.

Our daughter Anabella Persephone wailed and wailed in my grandmother's arms.

"Grandmother."

"Where are you going, Alessandro? She needs you."

"I am going to the Underworld to have a little chat with my mother," I growled.

"You don't think Persephone did this, do you?"

"I'm sure of it. You know how spiteful and cruel she can be," I answered.

"Be careful, Hades is likely to take her side."

"I know he will, but this isn't right. Anabel was young and vibrant. Death shouldn't have come for her. Not now."

"I know," my grandmother nodded. "Just tread carefully. Your father and mother aren't always the most forgiving of people."

"I don't care if they hate me, grandmother. I have to try to make this right. Please look after my daughter in my absence."

"Of course."

I walked straight down into the Underworld as if I owned the place.

"Well, well, look who came to visit?! If it isn't my little brother," Zagreus cackled.

I punched him in the face. I didn't have any regrets. I was too angry.

"Oh, someone's got a temper!" he shouted after me, laughing.

Evidently, the fact that I just punched him in the face didn't phase him, in the least. These were strange people, indeed. *How did I come from them?* I wondered.

My mother looked up at me slyly from beneath her heavily lidded blue eyes. She brushed white-blonde hair away from her face. "My darling boy, I haven't seen you in the Underworld for many moons. Come here, let Mother see you."

I am certain she could feel my pure, unadulterated loathing. My anger was hot beneath my skin.

Despite this, she saw the need to stroke her fingers through my white blonde hair, so like hers. I was her double except in male form. Perhaps, that's why she took such offense that I chose life instead of death like she had.

My father walked over, his long dark hair swaying behind him like a dark current of waves. His equally dark eyes looked me over, almost as if curious. "What brings you here, Alessandro?"

"I think you know what brings me here," I answered, barely managing to keep my voice at a level tone. "Anabel."

"Some people die young, my son," my mother crooned, clearly enjoying this. She wanted me to come down here. I realized this entirely too late. I had given her exactly what she wanted, which only further fueled my anger.

It wasn't enough that she had convinced my father to take my wife, she was purposefully provoking me.

"It's funny how no harm befell my Anabel until after you so nastily admitted your jealousy of her."

"Is it a sin for a mother to miss her son?"

"Of course not," I snapped. "But you see me every spring."

"Like that's enough," my mother argued.

"It's not my fault that you drove me away just like your mother drove you away," I responded, curtly.

"She's only a mortal girl, Alessandro, what are you getting so worked up about?" Melinoe asked.

"She had my heart," I shouted. Loudly enough that Cerberus bowed his head. He looked afraid, and that dog never seemed afraid of anything.

"Calm down," my mother insisted, smiling sweetly. It was a deception. I wasn't convinced. I knew she didn't mean it. "Perhaps, we can come to an understanding."

"Like what?" I demanded, coldly.

"You look like your father after I tell him he cannot see you when you make that face," my mother giggled.

I was far from amused, and she knew it. There was a devilish look in those blue eyes of hers.

"WHAT DO YOU WANT?!"

Cerberus whimpered.

"Now, now, Alessandro, let's not get too excited," my father insisted. "I know that you're upset—"

"That's the understatement of the century," I muttered, interrupting his statement entirely.

"Perhaps, we can work something out."

"What is it that you want?"

"Anabel can return to life if you stay here for six months."

"No strings attached?" I asked, suspicious.

"No strings attached," my father answered.

I was skeptical, but if being here six months meant that I could see my wife again then I would do it. What else could I do? I didn't like the idea of spending six months down here, but what more could I do? Humanity, I knew, would suffer in my absence. But six months worth of my personal suffering and they would have me back to help them.

Was it selfish to want something for myself for once?

"Agreed," I answered.

My mother's eyes danced with mirth that I knew couldn't mean anything good. "It'll be so nice to see you, my darling son. Do you think your daughter will remember you when you return? Do you think my mother will forgive you for this?"

"You're twisted," I retorted, recoiling from her. "How anyone can like you is beyond me."

"That's a little uncalled for," my father insisted, narrowing his eyes.

"And what *she* said to *me* wasn't?" I retorted. "You both may hate Demeter, but she's been nothing but good to me." I then turned my back on my parents, hating them for trapping me here. I knew they'd take advantage of me being here. I could feel it in the sick, perverted glee of my siblings.

***

When six months time was up, I was elated. I knew I needed to get away from these people or else I would forever lose my sanity.

"Before you go, you must do something for me," my mother remarked.

"I thought you said this was with no strings attached," I insisted to my father.

He shrugged as if words were meaningless and promises were moot to him. My mother must have gotten to him.

"You have never used your power to kill. Please use it now, and you can have your Anabel back."

"Never," I growled.

"Oh, come on. There must be some insect that doesn't deserve to live, some animal, perhaps even some wicked mortal ..."

"I promised I would never use that power," I shouted at her.

"Come, darling, you've already sacrificed six months and who knows how many mortals who have suffered in that time. What's one death?" she sneered.

I hated her, I hated her more than I have ever hated any winter or any death in my life. I knew I would regret this later, but I watched a tiny insect that harmed flowers fly into the garden. With one gesture of my hand, it was dead.

"See, that wasn't hard," my mother cackled.

My shoulders shook with my fury. "It wasn't right, either," I retorted. "Every living creature is simply trying to survive. What right should I have to take away their life to live?" I demanded. I glanced down at the soul of Anabel's in my arms. I hoped that she would forgive me.

"What a weakling!" Melinoe shouted from behind me.

"Valuing life isn't a weakness, Melinoe. It's actually one of his strengths," Macaria stated. "What mother did was both cruel and wicked, and I do not blame him for being angry."

I walked away, grateful that one of them understood me, at the very least.

When I returned to my grandmother's garden, I told her of everything that had happened, and I wept when I got to the end.

"Persephone will pay for that," my grandmother promised. "And Anabel will forgive you, I know she will," she insisted.

She wasn't wrong. When my love came to life, and I told her this story, looking away, she kissed my cheeks. "You are the sweetest, most selfless man I have ever known. You aren't going to use that power again, are you?"

"Never."

"Then don't be ashamed. They just put you in a bad position," she remarked. "But I am glad that your suffering wasn't all for naught. Now, where's our daughter?"

My mother never came that spring or the spring after that. I think she thought when she came up the spring after that perhaps my anger would have cooled. I didn't speak to her, at all, and nor did Anabel. We didn't give her a chance to see her granddaughter.

As far as I was concerned, Persephone wasn't my mother and Hades wasn't my father. I didn't need either of them in our lives. All I needed were my flowers, my trees, my grandmother, my wife, my daughter, and whatever future children my wife and I might have had.

Sometimes you have to rid toxic people from your life regardless of whether or not they're family.

Second Chances

Noah Daniels

A Day in The Life of The Son of Death

"You still haven't asked Mara out?" Darius asked.

Damon Powers blushed slightly as he tossed his rock at the lake. Six skips. Not bad at all.

"She's still dating Justin," Damon explained sheepishly.

Darius rolled his eyes and skipped his rock. Five skips. He cursed under his breath.

"Dude. You're not serious. That guy is a creep. He's no competition for you. Besides, wasn't she gonna break up with him?"

Damon sighed, sitting down on the rocks. Darius joined suit. Out of habit, Damon picked up a rock and transformed it into a can of Coke. He passed it to Darius and made one for himself.

"You know how Mara is. She's so easy to intimidate, and Justin intimidates her. Plus she's, you know. Grieving over you."

Darius made a sound that could have either been a quick laugh or a cough. He drank a sip of Coke and shook his head.

"How is everybody doing?" he asked quietly.

Damon took a moment before answering. He sipped his Coke and tried to think of a way to deliver the news lightly. The last thing he wanted was to make Darius feel guilty.

"Well. Mara is pretty messed up over it. So is Kyle. Your parents are … not good."

Darius sat up a little straighter.

"They're not bad off, are they?"

Damon spread his hands and shifted awkwardly.

"Well, it's just that Christmas is coming up. This is their first Christmas without you. All of ours, really. Not to mention you're their only son."

Darius was silent for what felt like forever.

"Death is complicated, Damon."

Damon shook his head.

"No, death is pretty straightforward. Life is the tricky part. In life, you lose people. In death, you're reunited."

"I guess that's fair. Still. My parents shouldn't have to deal with this. They shouldn't …" Darius' voice caught. His hand shook as he raised his can.

Damon gently set his hand on Darius' shoulder.

"Look, man. I get that this sucks. But your parents are so freaking proud of you. We all are too. Would you rather that kid's parents have to go through this?"

"No," Darius answered immediately, then shivered.

"No. Of course not. That's why you pushed him out of that street and got hit instead. You're a hero, Darius. The part we don't talk about is that heroes are usually tragic."

Darius sipped his Coke as a tear rolled down his cheek.

"And there's nothing we can do? You can't tell them that you see me every afternoon? You can't tell them I'm doing alright or anything?"

Damon took a deep breath.

"Darius, answer me one question. Until you died, did you know that I was the Son of Hades?"

Darius opened his mouth but then closed it.

"No."

"And how long did we know each other? Weren't we best friends?"

"That's not one question, man. That's three. But we knew each other most of our lives, and we are the best of friends."

"But I didn't tell you. I couldn't. I'm the son of Hades, and there's some stuff I can't do. I can't let on who I am. I can't tell people what to expect when they die. I can't bring people back to life."

"And you can't tell me what my reincarnation test will be," Darius added with a slightly annoyed tone.

Damon snorted and sipped his Coke.

"Nope. Can't do that either. All I can do is train with you and get you ready for it when it comes. And, you know, chill with you in

Elysium until then. Which isn't a bad way to hang out, I think."

"You say train with me. I call it getting my butt handed to me for three hours. I can't believe, after all these years of me taking up for you, you turn out to be freaking Chuck Norris."

Damon grinned, the kind of expression that betrayed a mischievous pride. It was not often that Damon got to show off his skills to anyone important. In the mortal world, he was forbidden from using the skills he learned in the Underworld. Unfortunately, there were not many teenage masters of combat that walked around in the mortal world.

"Nah, I mean, I'm glad you actually took up for me. You should be too because Dad really took notice of it. It wouldn't have been good for me to have fought for myself. People would have gotten seriously hurt."

Darius snorted, sipped his Coke, and looked up. His eyes narrowed a little bit.

"Um … Isn't that your stepmom's … uh … isn't that Adonis?" he asked.

Damon looked past Darius and saw the man he was talking about. He groaned loudly.

Have you ever seen a person who was so utterly good looking that it was honestly annoying? That was Adonis.

Damon had once asked his mother, whom he considered a person of excellent character, why she had dated a married man—married god?—and Persephone had responded, "She literally gets the best looking man who EVER lived for three months of the year. I don't think she was hurting," and that was fair. Adonis was the best-looking guy who ever lived. He had the annoying habit of walking around shirtless, and every muscle in his body rippled like a pond in a storm. His hair was indescribably perfect. His eyes changed depending on who was looking into them, to be the ideal of whoever looked. For most of the year, he was with Aphrodite, the goddess of love, but unfortunately, this time of year he was in the Underworld. He often played chaperone to the boy.

"Don?" Damon called.

Adonis hated being called that. He said it took the mystique out of his name.

"Hey, Dame," and Damon growled to himself because he had forgotten his stepmother's annoying nickname for him, "your father wishes to see you in the palace. It's almost time for you to go."

Damon sighed heavily and turned to Darius. The latter boy had a slight smile.

"Man, even if your dad's a god, you've still gotta listen to adults. Who'd have thought?"

Damon snorted as he got up.

"I'll be back tomorrow, bro. We'll train some more then. Who knows? Maybe you'll manage to skip a rock further than me this time."

Darius kicked Damon lightly, and Damon laughed.

"See you, Damon," Darius grunted.

"Adios."

Damon made his way up the shore to a waiting Adonis. The supernaturally attractive man raised an eyebrow.

"Can't help noticing you've been spending a lot of time with that boy. I shouldn't call for more … adult supervision, should I?"

Damon almost choked.

"God no! I'm into girls, Don. Besides, he's dead. That would be, like, five times as weird."

"Your stepmother shares a bed with the god of the Underworld. It's not like things like that can't happen."

Damon made a gagging sound.

"Don, I really don't need to hear about who my dad shares a bed with."

"She tells me things she likes, you know. I could give you details."

"Adonis, I swear to Zeus I'll kill you again if you keep going."

Adonis laughed, a sound like a bell choir. Gods he was annoying. The two proceeded along the Highway to Hell—no, that was not its original name. Yes, it was named for the song—and slowly to the Pandaemonium, the palace of the Underworld. From the highest tower, a loud bell played out a familiar melody.

Damon groaned when he realized the song was "Hell's Bells." Adonis began to hum along as the doors opened inwardly before them and a skeletal guard made up of Myrmidons, cavalry from the Khan Empire, and American Navy Seals suddenly surrounded them as an escort.

"I'll never understand why Hades only wants us guarded when we get to the palace," Adonis remarked.

Behind them, a Myrmidon began to unsheathe his sword. Damon smiled to himself.

"Hey, Adonis, behind you," he warned.

Adonis whirled and yelped, ducking a high stab from the Myrmidon. He swung, a clumsy roundhouse type of punch that any man with sight could dodge, and suddenly he and the Myrmidon were dancing around the obsidian floors of the palace.

Damon whistled to the rest of the guard, all of them smiling, and they proceeded without the two combatants. The floor before them opened up into steps that ascended to three levels. A purple velvet carpet rolled down all three levels, and the walls around were encrusted with the finest jewels and gemstones.

Before long Damon ascended the carpet and the final set of doors swung open. Damon stepped through the doors with his escort now behind him. Before him, sitting on a throne of bone and precious stone, sat his father, Hades. He was singing in a voice far too deep and far too out of key the lyrics to "Hell's Bells," which he presumably listened to through a set of Beats. Beside him, on a throne of pine wood and cedar, sat Persephone.

Damon had seen people being tortured in the Fields of Punishment once, having wandered too far on accident, and the look on their faces was reminiscent of Persephone's expression.

"I hate it when he tries to be modern," Persephone said to Damon as he entered.

Damon cringed as his father's voice cracked on a note that was out of his baritone range.

"He's still on that AC/DC kick?" he asked, the sympathy evident in his voice.

"I begged Apollo to introduce him to some new music, but Hades insists they're a classic. At the top of every hour, that godawful song plays on the bells. It's been stuck in my head since October. It's worse than when Beethoven died, and he kept making the poor man play the 'Moonlight Sonata' for a century."

"Sorry," Damon responded with feeling.

Persephone sighed.

"I'll live."

Hades suddenly ripped the arm bones off of his throne, and air drummed the last few beats of the song, screaming out the last notes. The escort guard shuffled back a few paces. Persephone rolled her eyes and rested her face in her open palm. Damon could take no more.

"DAD!" he yelled.

Hades, whose eyes had previously been closed, snapped open. When he did, his mouth formed a slight smile. It was not usually in the god's nature to smile brightly or warmly, given that he was usually dark and cold. Still, he did the best he could when he was with Damon.

"Ah! Damon, you're here. Good. Your mother was asking for you to come home, so I thought I would see you off."

The god, who was usually at least eight feet tall, stood from his throne and shrank to a more comfortable six-foot figure. He took off his Beats and gently placed them on the floor. His robe was wrinkled, and so Hades took a moment to straighten it. With that done, he spread his arms.

"Give me a hug before you leave, Damon. I see you so rarely," he invited.

"You see me every afternoon, from three to six. And every other weekend. How is that rare?"

Hades' smile flickered.

"When you live for a few thousand years, Damon, three hours and a few days feel like five minutes. Besides, lately, you've been spending all your time with Darius."

Damon acknowledged the point and went to his father, giving him the requested hug. Hades chuckled and released Damon after a moment.

"Gotta say, I like that Darius boy. He really has the soul of a hero. And of course, he's had my boy's back all these years."

Damon was about to respond, but suddenly a scream sounded, and a frantic man scurried into the throne room. Behind him, an angry Myrmidon with a drawn sword rushed in. Adonis ran toward a Navy SEAL and attempted to pry the man's sidearm free, but the SEAL hit him with an elbow and sent him staggering.

"GO AWAY, YOU STUPID SOLDIER!" Adonis shouted at the Myrmidon.

"What on earth?" Persephone yelled, immediately throwing an accusatory glance down at the now smaller Hades. Hades shot a furtive glance of sheer annoyance at Damon, then nodded to the Navy SEAL that had hit Adonis. The SEAL drew his sidearm and stepped out of ranks, shooting the Myrmidon down with it. Adonis, who had been running to the corner of the throne room, stopped and caught his breath.

"Thanks, soldier. I dunno what happened. I was with the kid and next thing I knew, that idiot attacked me. Damon was kind enough to warn me, but he did nothing else to help," Adonis then shot an angry look at Damon. Damon shrugged.

"I'm not supposed to use my powers," he responded nonchalantly.

"In the mortal world," Persephone corrected, glaring at Hades and Damon.

Hades shifted his feet awkwardly.

"Of course, we'll get to the bottom of this, Adonis. I've no idea what could have prompted this—"

"Mmhm," Persephone interjected.

"But it will not happen again." Hades coughed suddenly, but the cough sounded oddly like the words "for a while."

Adonis bowed.

"Many thanks, Lord Hades. You are a most gracious god. And I thank you, Damon, for so kindly warning me," Adonis shot a look at Damon that seemed to belie his thanks.

"Oh yeah. Anytime for you," and Damon almost managed to sound sincere.

Persephone had lost her focus on Hades and Damon, instead staring at Adonis. His hair was a tangle of Mediterranean curls now, and his jeans had been cut at the upper thighs to suggest that the Myrmidon had attempted most unkind cuts. A fair bit of flesh was exposed, and Persephone's eyes gleamed like Underworld diamonds.

"I'll just be attending to Adonis and his wounds. Damon, it was lovely seeing you," Persephone said airily before she and Adonis disappeared in a cloud of lily petals.

Hades gave Damon a bemused look.

"Why would you warn the moron?" he moaned.

"I figured he should at least get a sporting chance."

Hades gestured at the air around them and Persephone's empty throne.

"He's getting a sporting chance right now, it would seem. I so nearly had the tree born bastard."

Damon could not resist laughing at his dad's frustration. Hades made a sound of disgust.

"Yeah, yeah. Laugh it up. I only made sure your best friend got a streamlined process to Elysium but go ahead. Laugh at my frustration."

Damon suddenly remembered what he had been going to ask.

"About that. Dad, what exactly ... I mean, I know you can't tell me specifics, but what is

Darius gonna have to do if he tries for the Isles? What's the test like?"

Hades waved his hands as if to deflect the question.

"Damon, you know I can't divulge such information. The test is designed to show that he has not just the soul of a hero, but has the spirit to go back to the pains of the mortal world. That's all I can tell you. And of course, you know that if he passes, he will bathe in the River Lethe and lose his memories, only to regain them upon his next death. He has to do this three times to earn the Isles. That's all you can know."

Damon paused for a moment. The knowledge, which of course he had known, had never actually occurred to him as having any relevance.

"He … he has to lose his memory?"

Hades frowned.

"Of course, he does. Every hero who made it to the Isles had to. You've known that for years."

Damon stared at his father uncomprehendingly for a moment. At last, he forced some clarity into his eyes.

"Right. I knew that, of course."

Hades regarded Damon with what Damon thought was concern. It was always hard to read his father's emotions. He usually had so few of them.

"Go home to your mother, son. It does no mortal well to be so split between life and death," Hades adjoined.

He stepped aside then and extended his hand, moving it in a circular motion. As he did, darkness and shadows manipulated themselves into a circle, and then a transparent portal that showed Damon's kitchen.

"I'll see you tomorrow, right?" Hades asked.

"Yeah, of course. I have to keep training with Darius."

Hades nodded, satisfied, and Damon ran through the portal.

The Mortal World

Damon stepped out of the portal and was immediately struck by the smell of his mother's vegetable soup. The freshly mopped tile floor threatened to sweep Damon off his feet as he slid a few inches out of the portal. The next thing that reached his senses—after he had regained his balance at least—was the sound of The Doobie Brothers singing *Black Water*. His mother always said it reminded her of her childhood visits to Rocky River with her parents.

In Damon's mind, he saw the icy black waters of the River Styx with the broken promises that filled its current like shards of pearl. The last thing to greet him was the sight of his mother, Helena, stirring a large crockpot and quietly singing along to her iPod.

"Oh good, you're home. Dinner is almost ready," Helena greeted him.

"Cool, I'm freaking starving," Damon replied. He went to the cabinet and produced a bowl and plate for himself and then the same for his mother, setting both on the kitchen table. The song changed to Gordon Lightfoot, who began singing *Carefree Highway*. As he began to sing, a loud timer went off, promptly cutting Gordon off.

Helena whirled to turn the timer off, and the action sent her wavy, Nyx-black hair flying to the other side of her head. Helena had always been such a pretty woman. Damon could not say it aloud, lest his stepmother hear it, but he thought his mom was easily a prettier woman than Persephone. Helena opened the oven and pulled out a pan full of muffins.

"How is Darius?" Helena asked.

Helena Powers was the only mortal who knew that Damon was the son of Hades. She was a devout Catholic, which was complicated for obvious reasons, yet she always made sure she was aware of what went on in her son's supernatural life. This meant she was also the only other living mortal who knew that Darius was faring quite well as a hero in Elysium.

"He's alright. We trained for two and half hours or so and then we just hung out for the last bit."

Helena bit her lower lip, a habit she always resorted to when thinking.

"Well, that makes him better off than his parents. God help them, they're still a mess."

A knot formed in Damon's stomach.

"How bad are they?"

"Well, you know I try to call Donna as much as I can. I called her today to check on her, and she broke down about fifteen minutes into the call. She said they can't even bear the thought of decorating for Christmas this year. It was just pitiful. It broke my heart. Plus neither her nor Greg have gone back to work yet, but they'll have to soon."

Damon sighed.

"I know what you mean. Mara and Kyle aren't exactly holding up well, either. We were eating lunch yesterday, and Kyle just couldn't stop saying it's not the same. Mara looked like she was gonna cry the whole time. He finally caught on to that and stopped. What can I say to all of it? 'Guys, it's cool. Darius is chilling with Muhammed Ali and Perseus, son of Zeus, he's not hurting that much. I see him every day after school.'"

"Yeah, how is that going? Have they asked why you're not hanging out with them as much anymore after school?"

"Not really. I don't even think they hang out much now. Kyle goes home and throws himself into school work and reading and working on that history of Japan. Mara goes off to Justin and throws herself into him."

Helena grabbed a bowl and a ladle.

"Here, pour yourself some soup and get some muffins. There's cheese on that saucer and crackers. I made a glass of ice for you too. I just made some more sweet tea, it's in the fridge. It's full, be careful."

"Got it, thanks, Mom," Damon said, and he did as she said.

They reconvened at the table, each with their meals made up. Helena led them in grace.

"Bless us, O Lord, and these, Thy gifts, which we are about to receive from Thy bounty. Through Christ, our Lord. Amen."

Mother and son crossed themselves and began to eat. Behind them, on the counter, the genre shifted on Helena's iPod and John Coltrane began to play *Why Was I Born."*

"God, you and Dad have such different taste in music," Damon remarked.

Helena raised her eyebrows.

"Has he gotten past *Hooked On A Feeling* yet?"

Damon cracked up with laughter on hearing that.

"Oh yeah, he's on *Hell's Bells* lately. He's driving half the Underworld crazy with it. You know he got himself a pair of Beats?"

Helena said she did not, though it did not surprise her.

"Yeah, he was listening to the song on them. Someone really needs to tell him there are other bands to listen to."

Helena thought about that.

"I tried to get him to listen to Kiss once. He liked them, especially their look, but then he heard *God of Thunder* and got all pissed off."

"Anyone ever try to get him on Breaking Benjamin, Skillet, Evanescence—"

"Oh God, please no. Could you imagine him getting hooked on *My Immortal*? People all throughout the Underworld would try to kill themselves all over again," Helena interrupted him.

That made both of them laugh, and then dinner was quiet for a moment. Damon slurped some of his soup off his spoon, and once more was reminded how good it was. There was just enough spice in it to give it the perfect kick.

"Y'know, Mara wouldn't keep throwing herself into Justin, as you put it, if you'd just grow a pair and ask her out."

And then Damon found out what spicy vegetable soup tasted like as it came through his nose. He choked for about thirty seconds, then grabbed his sweet tea and drank it down to help.

"Mom!" he protested, sputtering out the word.

"Just sayin'," Helena shrugged.

"Well, how about some warning next time? How did you even—" Damon began to ask.

"Oh please. You ain't slick. You talk about her all the time. You have for years."

"I talk about all of my friends a lot!" Damon argued.

"Yeah, but if Kyle texts you, you take fifteen minutes to reply. If you realize that Mara texted you, I have seen you run faster than you can teleport to your phone. You're really obvious."

"You sound like Darius," Damon grumbled.

"Always liked him," Helena grinned, but a little wistfully.

Damon caught the difference.

"How are we going to try and help his parents?" he asked.

Helena exhaled deeply and shrugged.

"I dunno, Damon. I invited them to Mass with us, and Donna said she could definitely use some prayer so she'd see what Greg said. Other than that? I dunno. There's a word for kids who lose both their parents, but there's no word for parents who lose a child. You can't describe that pain, and you can't take it away."

"Maybe if you cleared their memories," Damon muttered bitterly.

Helena frowned.

"What are you talking about?"

Damon silently cursed. He should not have said that. Why he should not have said it, he was not really sure. Something told him, instinctively, it was a bad move in a game he was not aware he had been playing. Still, it was his mother he said it to. He could, and usually did, tell her anything.

"Darius. If he goes for reincarnation and passes his test, he'll have to wash in the River Lethe before he can come back to life."

Helena sat back, away from her meal.

"Right. He'll lose his memories of this life and won't get them back until he dies again. I thought you know that. Even I knew that."

Damon clenched a fist in frustration under the table.

"I did know that. It's just ... I never thought that Darius would have to do it, y'know? It's like ... You know that in football you're more likely to get a concussion, right? But you never really think your best friend the quarterback is gonna end up out for the season because he got a really bad concussion in the first game. That happens to other people, not the people ..." and here Damon trailed off.

Helena smiled sympathetically.

"Not the people you know and are close to. Trust me, Damon, I get it. You never think of a boy you watched grow up getting killed by saving a kid in the street. As a mother, I always worry about the worst happening to you, but to your friends? But it happens, and there's nothing you can do to change it."

Damon thought about that. *Nothing you can do to change it.* The words seemed to echo in his ears. Suddenly, they stopped bouncing around and began to take root instead.

"Yeah. I guess so," Damon sighed.

Helena regarded him for a moment, and unlike Hades, the concern on her face was clear.

"Are you okay?" she asked.

"Yeah, yeah I'm fine. I mean, who knows? Darius may not even pass the test. Even if he does, he'll be alive again. Maybe ... Maybe we'll cross paths again," Damon said hesitantly, and Helena smiled once again.

She took another bite of soup and crunched on her last cracker, and Damon was happy for the end of those questions.

"How much homework do you have?" Helena asked, this time much more casual.

"Not much. I got most of it done in school," Damon replied.

Helena nodded, used to hearing that quasi-truthful statement. She knew that half the time it was a lie, and that really Damon was going to do most of it in the morning or at lunch, but it got done and usually with high marks. If he wanted to screw himself over, then that was his prerogative.

"Alright. Help me clean the kitchen, then go and take care of your homework. Want to watch TV at nine? A new Goldbergs came on this week."

"Sure," Damon responded.

Thirty minutes later he was in his room, rifling through his bookshelf. I know, who actually reads hard copy books anymore, right? More to the point, what kind of teenager has books like The Odyssey, The Iliad, Telemachus: The Mysterious Myth, Ovid's Metamorphoses, and The Golden Ass (by Apuleius, not Hugh Hefner)? These are fair questions, but it must be understood that things change when you are the son of a Greek god. By design, you become a little more old-fashioned. Not to mention, for the majority of us, Greek myths are simply ancient stories whose gripping adventures and marvelous writing grip us. When you are the son of Hades, they become very informative books that pertain very much to your life. And so Damon flipped through the pages of the poets, searching for a clue, a hope, anything that could help him. There was nothing. Many poets and philosophers had described Lethe, each with varying degrees of accuracy. Virgil most accurately attested that one must drink from the river before being reincarnated. Statius correctly said it bordered Elysium. None of this was helpful though, and eventually, Damon growled in frustration and flung Ovid's work across the room.

"Algebra homework?" Helena called.

"Not tonight, no," Damon called back with a note of agitation.

He flopped down on his bed and ripped his phone from his pocket and fumbled with it, trying to untangle his earbuds and in the process lost his grip. The phone fell and smacked Damon on the forehead. Damon swore fervently and snatched his phone from his face, ripped his earbuds out of their socket and flung them across the room next. He tapped the Safari button with the fervor of a punch and pulled up Google.

Cursing the Lethe, Damon searched the River Lethe on the search engine. *May the gods bless Wikipedia,* Damon thought and tapped that option. He scrolled for a moment, increasingly growing agitated by what he saw. Then he saw something that triggered a vague memory.

Mnemosyne.

Damon's eyes widened. Yes, he had heard that word before. It was a distant memory, something that he remembered his father telling him about once. It was not one of the rivers of the Underworld, he knew that. There were only five of those, and he had seen all of them. However, the memory he had and the words on the article went together. The Mnemosyne had the power to restore all a person's memories, even of their past lives.

Then an idea began to formulate. It was a crazed, incredibly far-fetched idea, but the thought of it made him smile like Boris Karloff's Grinch. He was so deep inside his own mind that when his phone vibrated he nearly jumped from his bed.

"Who is texting ..." Damon grumbled, frustrated to have his scheming interrupted.

Then he saw who was texting him. His heart did an odd tap dance, which was the usual result of seeing that Mara had texted him. His hands, only a moment ago dry and capable, were now grubby with sweat. The message was seemingly a simple one, but in the world of teenage romance, *simple* does not seem to exist.

"Hey Damon, can you get to school a little earlier tomorrow? I really need to talk to you about something."

Damon's grubby thumbs punched the keys as fast as they could move.

"What time? 8:00?"

The dreaded three dots appeared on his screen, indicating she was typing. Damon set his phone on the bed and paced the floors, trying to anticipate her next message. He would glance at his phone every few seconds, but still, the dots were there. After a minute they vanished, and Damon nearly screamed "Don't toy with me!" when suddenly her reply appeared.

"Maybe 7:50? I know it's early, but it's private and I don't know who else to talk to."

Damon did a little skip. That meant she chose him over Kyle. Moreover, it meant she was talking to him and not Justin. Maybe, oh could it be, there was trouble in the purgatory that was their relationship? In his mind, Damon had an image of Mara confessing her profound love for him.

Watch it be something about Greek mythology for English, Damon's more cynical nature whispered to him.

Shut up, the optimistic side ordered.

"Yeah, I can do that. Is everything okay?"

Once again, the three dots. It is well known that those three dots have caused young boys to go gray from stress, and this moment was no different.

"We'll talk tomorrow morning. Thanks so much Damon, you're a great friend."

Damon's skipping heart suddenly sank beneath the icy waters of the River Styx. *Friend.* That word had gunned down and crucified the romantic hopes of men for generations. He glanced at the time on his phone. 8:45 p.m.

"It's no problem. See you tomorrow :)" Damon replied, and the smile was a strategic play. It would show he was happy to be there for her.

With that dreadful conversation done, Damon groaned and tossed his phone onto his bed. It was close enough to nine, and God knew he could stand a final hour of TV before the next day.

Mara

Damon Powers often woke up before the sun was up; as a son of the Underworld, he was prone to enjoying the darkness. As such, arriving at school early was hardly an imposition. By six-thirty, Damon had showered, eaten breakfast, gotten dressed, done his homework for the day, and was now pacing the floor of his room with a major case of nerves.

It's funny the things that confound people. Damon had been taught to fight by the world's greatest warriors and heroes. By the time he was five, he could handle a sword against Leonidas of Sparta. By age seven, he could outshoot Genghis Khan on horseback. By thirteen, it took Heracles a few minutes before he could pin Damon—after all, no lean muscled kid was going to outperform the strongest man to ever live—and by sixteen Damon was sparring Bruce Lee for hours. Yet, though Damon was fearless in the face of a bodily threat, he was terrified of talking to a girl with whom he had been friends since middle school. It was the first semester of their senior year, so Damon knew time was running out if he wanted to tell Mara how he felt.

But that was not all that gnawed at his mind.

His crazy plan flickered through his mind like an ember that refused to be put out. He knew that it would take a crazy amount of luck to accomplish it, but maybe the Fates would be kind enough to spot him that luck. Once again, his thoughts were interrupted by the sound of his door opening. Damon jumped once more.

"Oh! Sorry, didn't mean to startle you," Helena apologized.

Damon took a deep breath.

"It's alright. Sorry, I'm a little jumpy this morning."

"I can tell. I'm heading off to confession. There anything you want to confess to me about why you're up and pacing earlier than normal?"

Damon blushed and stuttered out something about how he could not sleep. Helena smiled broadly.

"It's Mara, isn't it?"

"Yep."

"That's awesome, hon! What did she say?"

"She just asked me if I could come to school early and talk. She said it's important, but she wouldn't tell me what it was about."

Helena pursed her lips.

"I hope everything is alright. She's such a vulnerable girl. You must mean a lot to her if she is willing to tell you about it in private. Don't be stupid."

"Thanks for the faith, Mom."

"It's what I do. Anyway, I'm running late. I'll tell Father Anthony you said hello."

"Thanks, Mom."

"Good luck," Helena added with a wink, and then hurried out of the apartment.

Damon decided to kill the next hour with music, and so he began to listen to some of his rock and metal while avoiding AC/DC like the plague. After listening to a bit of Breaking Benjamin's *Dear Agony* album, he decided seven-forty-five was good enough. He began to circle his hand, and as he did, the shadows of his room flew into a spiral that turned into an image of a stall in the boy's bathroom at school, near the media center.

Damon stepped through the portal and out of the stall, then checked his phone again. 7:48. Damon swung his bag over his shoulders and proceeded to make his way to the media center. In the recent past, the media center was where Damon, Darius, Mara, and Kyle would all meet in the mornings. It was there that they swapped stories and hid away from all the people who hated and disdained them, which was most of the school. Darius had been an odd exception. Darius was an athlete and well liked in the school, so in his case, people had been more confused by his choice in friends than disdainful of it.

The truth was that Darius and Damon had been friends since elementary school, and it never mattered to Darius how weird Damon and his other friends were. A friend of Damon was a friend to Darius. It had been beneficial for the others. So long as Darius was with them, nobody explicitly gave them crap. Now that he was gone? It was worse for all of them than it had been in years. Since Darius had died, to escape and group together before the day, the outcasts met in the media center as they did before. Still, things were not the same. Damon regretted this, yet at this moment it was lost on him. Mara had wanted to talk. He pushed the door to the media center open, strode through the scanner, and walked to the couch in the back where they usually sat. Kyle normally did not get to the school until 8:20, so they had about thirty minutes. 7:50.

Sure enough, as Damon sat down on the couch, the door opened once more, and Mara walked in. Damon gulped quietly when she did. She was clearly upset, but that did not take away from her looks. Her naturally dark brown hair was pushed back behind her ears, and her feminine figure was a little more prominent that day, in light of her black T-shirt, leather jacket, and gray skinny jeans. Her hazel eyes were downcast, and that made Damon focus. They were here to talk, not for him to gawk.

Don't be stupid, Helena spoke in his ears. He instinctively moved aside on the couch to make sure Mara had room to sit down, and then he took off his backpack. Mara took hers off as she came near, then flung it to the foot of the couch. She sat down beside Damon, and his heart began that tap dance once again.

"Hey," he greeted quietly.

They were the only two in the room, but just in case, he was quiet. It was apparently private, after all.

"Hey," Mara responded, just as quietly.

They sat for a moment in the silence, and the silence was deafening. Damon nearly spoke about a dozen times, but each time he stopped.

She wanted to talk to him.

He would not make her talk before she was ready. He knew by now it did no good.

Finally, Mara looked up and made eye contact with Damon. He knew that look; it was a look of deep, isolated pain that she had shown him in the past. He held his breath, knowing what came next even as she pushed up her left sleeve. A boulder materialized in his throat as he saw the new wound beside the old scars. Horizontal still, thank God, but still, it was a fresh wound. He stared at it for a second, and then he looked back into those hazel eyes. Green on the edges, flecks of brown towards the center. Tears on the lower lids.

"What happened?" he asked in a whisper.

Mara sniffed, then lowered her sleeve. One tear rolled down her cheek.

"Justin and I got in a fight last night."

Damon's blood slowed down and lost its heat. His veins seemed to turn to ice.

"What did he do?" he hissed.

Mara sniffed and wiped the tear from her cheek.

"He ... he had come off of a high an hour before. He gets so angry when he first comes off. And he gets so ... He wanted to make out, and I didn't want to. I had checked Facebook, and I saw someone had posted on Darius' wall ... It just messed me up, y'know? I didn't want to do that. Not then."

"You had every right," Damon said after a moment's hesitation.

Mara closed her eyes and wiped them vigorously. When she opened them again, they were slightly red.

"He accused me of loving a dead punk more than him."

"He did what?" Damon growled like a feral animal.

"I went off on him, Damon. I called him everything but a tree humper. I shouldn't have, I knew how angry he was, but ... It was Darius."

Damon stared into her eyes. He knew what she was going to say, he knew what should never have to be told was going to be revealed. Mara knew he had caught on. She lifted her shirt, an action that should have stunned Damon, yet he found he could not care about that action. He only cared about the fist-sized bruise on her abdomen. His veins were glaciers then.

"I didn't know what to do. I hit him with a book and ran," she whispered.

Damon moved swiftly, instinctively, and put his arm around Mara's shoulders. He drew her to his side, and she shed her tears on his shoulder.

"Did he come after you?"

"No. Knowing him, he probably finished himself off. He could've put a hole in the wall with that thing when he was trying to make out with me."

That was more than Damon wanted to know, but at least she had not been hurt again.

"Ditch that creep," Damon whispered in her ear.

Mara sniffed again.

"I know it's messed up, Damon, but I ... he's consistent. After Darius ... You just want to hold on to things."

"Hold on to me and Kyle, Mara. We're your friends, and we always will be. But that jerk deserves to die, not to date you."

Mara was quiet then. Damon sighed heavily; as he did, several muscles tensed. Mara had experienced a rough life. When she was in the seventh grade, her older brother had died suddenly. He went out to the yard to meet his friends and collapsed on the spot. After that, her parents had divorced, unable to cope well enough to stay together. Mara ended up with her mother, and the two of them moved into their current home. Mara had started as a new student in Damon's middle school, and she had never managed to fit in well. She had met Damon there, who, due to his father's blood, was always an outcast, understood her trouble. When Damon introduced her to Darius, she immediately became a close friend of the pair.

Still, she had kept cutting, and Damon and Darius had grown quite familiar with her scars. She had stopped in the eighth grade.

"Damon, how are you holding up so well? Out of everyone who knew him, you are handling him being gone the best. How? Don't you miss him?"

Damon swallowed hard. This was perhaps the most difficult part of his life, lying to his friends. He made up his mind to avoid lying. Mara needed something good to hold on to.

"Of course I miss him being here with us. Darius has been my friend for most of my life. But now that he's gone, I know he's in a good place. I know he'd want us to live our lives.

Mara looked up, making eye contact once more.

"I sometimes forget you're religious. So what? You think Darius is in Heaven?"

Damon regarded her for a moment.

"Where do you think he is?"

Mara considered the question.

"I think ... if there is a heaven, then Darius must have gotten in immediately."

Damon smiled wistfully.

"Immediately. Right."

Mara was quiet for a long time.

"Damon?"

"Yeah?"

"If Darius is in heaven, then we must be in hell. This life sucks."

Death is easy. Life is complicated, Damon remembered telling Darius.

"It's definitely more complicated," he admitted.

The door opened to the media center. Mara sat up straight away, and Damon leaned to the side, resting his arm on the couch armrest. The person who had entered was a stockier Asian kid with pale skin, which made him fit with Damon and Mara. He wore glasses and, like Damon, wore his oily hair long, to the shoulder. His trenchcoat was bogged down by his bookbag, which Damon knew would feature therein a Blue Exorcist manga, likely the lengthy volume Hirohito's War, and notes on a book about the history of Japan. The boy raised an eyebrow and looked back and forth between Mara and Damon.

"Am I interrupting something?" he asked.

Damon prayed he would not blush.

"No, Kyle, everything is status quo."

Kyle's eyebrows climbed even higher up his face.

"So then why did I just see Justin go by here looking like he wanted to nuke this school and muttering, 'I'll kill that punk'?"

Mara groaned, and Damon grinned mirthlessly.

"We were talking about Darius, and Mara got a little upset, so I brought her to me. You know. A friendly thing to do. I guess he saw it and thought it was more than friendly."

Kyle nodded. That made sense in light of recent weeks. He opened his mouth to speak once more, but the bell rang suddenly. Kyle glanced up, bewildered.

"Already?" he asked.

Damon shrugged.

"Guess so. See y'all at lunch?"

"As always," Mara sniffed, a smile now breaking the mask.

***

Lunch came too late as always, but things were different this day. As usual, Damon, Mara, and Kyle sat outside the cafeteria at a perforated table. It was a small number of people who sat outside, even though they were sheltered by an overhang held up by brick pillars. Damon had just sat down beside Mara with a styrofoam tray full of food when Kyle frowned. Through the window paneled wall, he saw something he did not like.

"Um. Guys?" he pointed through the window.

Damon and Mara turned around to see what he was talking about. When they did, they were not exactly ecstatic.

"Oh God," Mara said quietly.

Damon stared unflinchingly as Justin came closer and closer, then stepped through the door. This guy was an odd mixture. He was a little on the punkish side, often favoring dark clothes and heavy rock, but also an athlete. His build was like a college linebacker; he was all lean muscle, filling out his black T-shirt. His blond hair was usually gelled, and today was no exception; it hardly moved at all in the breeze when he stepped out. He saw Damon and Mara sitting together, and when he did, his breath came out steamy in the cold air.

"You little whore," he snarled at Mara.

Mara's eyes widened at the address.

Damon's blood went cold on hearing it.

Kyle began to get up, some degree of martial instinct coming to the forefront.

"Justin, listen to me," Mara began.

"Shut up! I'm not even surprised. First, you were hoeing around with that idiot Darius, and now you're with this scrawny little bastard."

"Justin!" Kyle snapped.

Justin looked at Kyle more attentively, then snorted.

"Sit down, Kyle. Nobody but these two ever talked to you in this school, and I'm not about to start."

Kyle's eyes narrowed, but he did not move. Justin was satisfied with this, now focusing on Damon. At this point, Damon stood up and turned to face the boy. *That's all he is*, Damon thought, *a boy*.

"You think you're something, huh? You stole my girl, MY GIRL, and sit with her like it's no big deal? You think you're just that cool, huh?"

"You should smoke another blunt, Justin. Calm down," Damon spoke quietly.

Justin's nostrils widened.

"And now you think you're Kevin Hart or something, making jokes."

"I'm serious. Smoke a blunt. Snort some coke. Whatever it is you do to keep calm, do it."

Justin stared at Damon, and now so did Mara. Damon had never said much when a jerk had started something with him. Seeing him like this, bold and unwavering, was the furthest thing from normal.

"Mara, get up. Come sit with me," Justin snapped.

"I'm not going anywhere with you. Not after last night," Mara shot back.

"What happened last night?" Kyle interjected, confused, but nobody bothered to answer him. Slowly, it dawned on the boy what could have happened. His fists clenched.

Justin snorted at Kyle's question, but his eyes never left Damon. Damon, meanwhile, kept staring into Justin's green eyes. They flashed like exploding emeralds.

"I guess I can't blame you for taking Mara on. After all, it must have been nice for somebody to want you."

"Justin! That's enough," Mara raised her voice.

"I mean, after all, your boyfriend did just get himself killed. You didn't have anybody else, other than this lame punk," Justin indicated Kyle with his left hand.

"Better him than someone like you," Damon replied casually.

Justin's eyes narrowed.

"Nobody likes you, man. Don't you know that? Even your dad couldn't deal with you. He knocked up your slut mom, then he realized he made a mistake like you and ran off. He left you to be the little bastard you are today."

Mara's jaw fell slack, as did Kyle's. Both looked as though they wanted to kill Justin, but both were too shocked that anybody could say such a thing. Damon, quite to the contrary, smiled. It was not a friendly smile; it was more like when chimpanzees bare their teeth in a smile as a threat. With that smile came a look of pure superiority, the smug look of a god.

"All that, and yet Mara wants me instead of you," Damon replied.

Justin yelled and swung at Damon, who ducked underneath the punch and hopped away from his seat, finally free to move. Justin whirled to face Damon, shocked to see his victim move so swiftly. Damon's smile broadened. Justin rushed him, closing the distance between them in a split second. His athletic prowess had come to play. Damon pretended to panic, jumping this time toward the nearest brick pillar. Justin did just as Damon hoped, throwing out his left arm and snagging Damon by the throat. With a loud grunt, Justin flung Damon backward into that pillar. Once more he closed in, grabbing Damon by the throat and pinning him. A heavy haymaker clubbed Damon in the jaw, only just managing to turn his head.

"I'll freaking rip you apart," Justin growled.

Damon's smile left him, it having accomplished its purpose. Justin was furious, and his thoughts were incoherent. Damon, on the other hand, was more focused than ever. Many guys have experienced what it is for their blood to turn to magma in their rage, but

Damon's blood was like a glacier. It was as cold as the waters of the Styx, yet sharp as an icicle.

"If you ever hit her again, I'll make sure you spend a thousand years in hell," Damon spoke, just loud enough for Justin to hear.

And then he fought back.

In the prime of his fame, Bruce Lee had cemented a reputation as being a master martial artist. One of his most famous attacks was the inch-punch, a punch he delivered from an inch long distance that could send his opponent flying. Though it has been studied by several martial artists, a small number can perform the punch as well as Bruce Lee could.

Damon Powers, having learned the punch from Bruce Lee himself in the Underworld, was one of those people. He moved swiftly, almost imperceptibly, and punched Justin at full force in the solar plexus.

Justin was launched backward, his back smacking against the concrete ground and his head following suit. There was a loud thwack! After this, Justin did not get back up. Instead, his chest rose and fell slowly. Mara and Kyle stood, slack-jawed, unable to comprehend what they had just witnessed. Damon nonchalantly brushed himself off, then turned to face Mara.

"I don't think he's gonna bother you anymore," he said cheerfully.

Before his friends could say anything, the door to the cafeteria burst open. A school administrator stood in the doorway, taking in the scene before them. First, he looked at the still standing students. Then he noticed the one on the ground. He looked back and forth between the two scenes, then directed his focus on Damon.

"Office. Now."

***

Damon sat for a long time on the uncomfortable couch in the office, waiting for his mother to get there. Normally, if students got into a fight, standard procedure was to simply have the students come into the office so as to figure out the circumstances and then dispense punishment. In this case, since Justin had been knocked out, Damon's parents were wanted present for the meeting.

The punishment could prove to be much more severe. The school receptionist would look up from her typing on occasion, see Damon, and shake her head in disgust. Damon hardly cared. Justin had hit Mara. He hit Justin harder. So far as he was concerned, he had dispensed justice.

That fearlessness fell apart when Helena walked into the office. Damon knew his mother would not take kindly to his getting in a fight. It might be different if she knew that Justin had hit Mara, but Damon had already resolved to keep that a secret. Mara had only told him, and he would not betray her trust. This meant he would have to withstand his mother's rage, which was evident in the glowering look she shot Damon.

"A fight?" she hissed.

"Mom," Damon began, a tremor suddenly taking his hands.

"A FIGHT?" she asked again, more loudly.

"It's not what you're thinking," Damon began, but it was clear already that by the time Helena was through with him, Hades would have full custody of him.

"Helena, please. We should give the boy a chance to explain himself," a deep voice called behind Helena.

Damon's blood chilled on hearing the voice. *There's no way*, he thought. But, as it turns out, there was.

Hades stepped into the office then.

Damon was too stunned to speak. He had never seen his father outside of the Underworld. He was suited black on black, with a blood red tie and his jacket unbuttoned. His oily black hair was pulled back in a ponytail, and a scraggly black beard had grown on his face. He eyed Damon with a mixture of intrigue and annoyance.

"Dad?" Damon breathed.

Hades sighed.

"Indeed."

Helena whirled on Hades with a fiery look.

"Indeed. Do you not care that your son broke our rules and got into a fight?"

"I think you're forgetting some of the things my family has been known to do," Hades responded dryly.

"Ms. Powers?" the principal called, stepping out of his office. His eyes widened when he noticed the strikingly tall figure of Hades. The principal, Ryan Stegall, cleared his throat.

"Excuse me, sir, can I help you?" he stammered.

Hades raised his hand in a calming gesture.

"Yes, sorry to drop in unannounced. I am Damon's father, Shadow."

The principal glanced at Helena, confusion etched on his face, but her expression confirmed it.

"Of course ... Right. All of you, please come in."

Hades stepped aside and gestured toward the door.

"Damon, Helena. After you."

Helena gave Damon the evil eye, and the boy knew better than to argue. He walked into Ryan's office, with Helena and Hades following suit. Damon took the seat across from the principal's desk, while Ryan pulled up chairs for Hades and Helena. Ryan took his seat in a leather rolling chair, then rubbed his eyes. Clearly, situations like fights were not his cup of tea.

"Damon, I must say. I am shocked at your behavior. Up until this moment, all I knew of you was that you are polite and intelligent. Your name never came before my desk unless it was to be on the Honor Roll. Now I have you in here to explain a fight. What do you have to say for yourself?"

Damon could not deny the nervousness that came from sitting between his parents. He could feel their eyes on him, and it sent a chill up his spine. Then he remembered Mara's bruise. The ice returned to his blood.

"He deserved it," Damon replied casually.

Ryan leaned back in his chair, and it was as though he could feel his hair turning gray.

"Okay then. Let's try a different approach."

Ryan turned his laptop around, revealing the security camera footage that showed the confrontation.

"Let me play this for your parents, so they know what exactly happened."

"Please do," Helena snapped.

It all took place before their eyes then. Damon was surprised to feel that surge of godly pride again as he watched Justin surge towards him. He saw himself jump aside. The angle did not allow for the baiting smile to be shown, but he knew when it happened.

Helena, despite her anger towards Damon, made a small sound of disgust when Justin seized Damon and flung him into the pillar. Hades cracked a grim smile, seeming to read Damon's lips as he issued the threat, but how he could possibly register that was beyond Damon. The video quality was far from stellar. When Justin was launched backward, Helena shook her head.

Still, Damon thought he could sense a tinge of pride beneath all of the more apparent anger.

Ryan paused the footage, then leaned forward. "It's quite clear that Justin attacked you first, and it's quite clear what you did to him. Now, what I want from you is to tell me what happened to cause this.”

“Damon, if this was justified, I want to know,” Helena urged.

Hades sat silently, teepeeing his fingers and turning to regard Damon. Damon sat for a moment, trying to figure out what he was going to say. Mara had only told him about Justin hitting her. She had said it was private. At that moment, Damon decided he would die before he betrayed her trust.

“Well?” Ryan pressed.

“We were fighting over Mara,” Damon replied. It was true, just not the entire truth.

“Oh for God’s sake,” Helena groaned.

Ryan raised his hands.

“Let’s remain calm, please.”

“You were fighting over a girl?” Hades asked, and skepticism dripped from his voice.

Damon shifted uncomfortably in his seat.

“Yeah … Yeah, we were.”

“You realize you can be suspended or expelled for fighting, Damon? It’s your senior year for God’s sake! You just ruined it over a stupid pissing contest?”

“Calm, please,” Ryan urged, but he had never seen Helena angry.

“Helena, let the boy explain his actions. I want to know what he was thinking,” Hades interjected.

“He wasn’t, Shadow!” Helena hissed.

“Helena. Let me clear some things up. Is that okay, Principal Stegall?” Hades responded with steely calm.

"Of course," Ryan stammered.

"How long has Mara been with this boy?" Hades asked.

"Two months," Damon replied mechanically.

Hades nodded slowly.

"Two months and you fight over her now? Why?"

Damon's stomach tightened. Hades was on to something. Without much thought, Damon realized he would have to use what he had told Kyle that morning.

"I was comforting her because we had been talking about Darius. Justin misconstrued that when he saw it."

"Then why didn't you try to set the record straight?"

Damon saw where this was going.

"I tried," he lied.

Hades raised an eyebrow.

"And he still swung at you?"

"He's a jackass," and that was true.

Hades kept a straight face, but Damon caught a slightly amused light in the god's eyes. Still, he pressed on.

"So he deserved the hospital for being a jackass, as you phrased it? That's not the Damon I know speaking."

Ryan cleared his throat.

"While I appreciate your input, Mr ..."

"Just Shadow will be fine," Hades clarified.

"Shadow. Well, I am glad to see parental involvement in such a pressing issue, but I would like to bring some other information to the table."

Helena sat forward.

"What kind of information are we talking about?"

"Well, as we were waiting for the two of you to come, we also interviewed the witnesses. Mara explained to us, rather tearfully, that Justin hit her last night. She showed us the bruise on her stomach and said that she confided to Damon today about it. Apparently, he comforted her, and this is what Justin saw. He then confronted your son, and the rest of the video took place. The other boy, Kyle, he also testified that Justin had alluded to hitting Mara in the confrontation. According to them, your son was defending Mara."

Helena's head whipped to Damon.

"Is this true?" she demanded.

Damon winced, then focused on Ryan.

"She ... she told you Justin hit her?"

Ryan smiled sympathetically.

"Looks like your friend wanted to defend you, too."

Helena's eyes welled up, and Hades smiled proudly.

"I knew it. I knew Damon wouldn't do something like that for no reason."

Ryan nodded.

"So it would seem. As such, taking into account the circumstances surrounding the fight and the fact that Damon was attacked first, it seems fitting that Damon should not be punished. I'll send him home with you today so that he can rest."

"He's not getting punished?" Helena asked, slightly surprised.

Ryan smiled mischievously.

"I can see why you'd think he may be, but no. He's done nothing wrong, and since I decide punishment, he gets what he deserves. Rewarded."

"May I ask why we were brought in, then?" Hades inquired.

Ryan tilted his head to regard Hades.

"I thought you should know your son is a hero. Now, before he leaves, I was asked to do someone a favor."

Ryan picked up the phone on his desk and dialed a short number.

"Excuse me, Mrs. Ephraim, can I borrow Mara for a moment? No, not Sarah. Mara. Yes, yes, that's the one. Great, thank you," he hung up and sighed.

"Really need a better intercom system," he grumbled.

Helena gave a laugh of relief, rising from her chair. Hades and Damon followed suit, Hades with a satisfied smile and Damon in a state of stupefied wonder. In a few moments, Mara appeared in the office. Her face betrayed her surprise when she saw the whole family, especially Hades.

"Damon? Are you okay? You're not in trouble, are you?" she blurted.

"No, I'm good," Damon smiled sheepishly.

Helena moved swiftly to the girl, pulling her into an emotional hug. Mara understood, having known Helena for years, what was intended. She returned the hug, yet could not take her eyes off of Damon and Hades. Helena pulled away and shot Damon a quick look, then stepped out of the office. Hades stepped forward then, extending a hand to Mara.

"You must be Mara. I'm Damon's father, Shadow."

Mara's eyes bulged, but she took the hand and shook it.

"It's nice to meet you, sir," she replied mechanically.

Hades nodded, and a sympathetic smile cracked across his face.

"I am truly sorry for all you've been through."

With that said, Hades too stepped out of the office. Ryan got up and twisted from side to side, stretching his lower back. He grunted when he straightened.

"Time to go to fourth lunch. Gotta make sure no fights break out and all that," he said ironically, then took his leave. Before he stepped out, he turned back. "Five minutes," was all he said.

Mara took a deep breath and looked into Damon's black eyes.

"Your dad seems—" she began.

"He's different, like us. But he's an awesome dad," Damon finished.

Mara shook her head in wonder. Damon had never mentioned his dad, and she had never asked. Actually meeting him was far from expected. Still, she regained her bearings quickly.

"Thank you," she whispered.

Damon struggled to find words that could get past that pesky boulder in his throat.

"Anything for you," he finally managed.

She did not say anything else. She just ran to him and threw her arms around him in a near suffocating hug. Damon rocked backward from the unanticipated collision, but before long he wrapped his arms around her, too. They stood for what felt like an eternity in the embrace until Damon eyed the clock in the office. Their five minutes were up. He moved to disentangle himself, and Mara understood. She pulled back, blushing slightly.

"You've gotta go, right?" she asked.

"Yeah ... I'll text you or call you, something, later."

"How about I just see you tomorrow?" Mara asked.

"Tomorrow is Saturday," Damon replied, confused.

Mara shook her head in bewilderment.

"I know that, Damon. How about I see you, tomorrow, at your house?"

Damon realized what was being asked and resisted the urge to smack his forehead.

"Yeah. We can do that."

Mara smiled warmly and walked outside of the office. She did have a class to get back to, after all. Damon stood, staring out the doorway, and then walked outside. Helena stood at one side, and Hades stood at the other. Helena raised her eyebrows.

"So I should expect company tomorrow?" she remarked dryly.

"Seems that way," Damon responded with faux nonchalance.

Hades turned to Helena.

"Helena, may I take the boy with me for the afternoon? It's nearly that time."

"Sure. And, Hades," Helena shot the god a smile, "it was good to see you. Thanks for coming to check on our son."

Hades shuffled his feet awkwardly.

"Of course," he mumbled, and Helena laughed. She left then, leaving only Hades and Damon. Hades cleared his throat.

"Shall we?"

Damon nodded, and as there was no one else in the office, Hades whisked them away.

The Crazy Idea

It was 5:20 pm, and that meant it was nearly time for Damon's crazy plan. He crouched behind a rock, near the shore of the River Styx. Training and talking with Darius had been a three-hour matter. Darius was certainly improving; he managed to land a few punches on Damon's torso, a few low kicks to his legs. This time, when they had finished, Damon had a slight limp to go with Darius's hobble. The best part had been when Damon related his adventure of the day to Darius.

"Holy crap! You actually knocked him out?"

"Oh yeah. That dude sailed," Damon had grinned mischievously.

Darius had high fived his friend.

"And you're seeing her tomorrow?"

"So it would seem."

"Don't you dare take advantage of her. You know she's vulnerable."

"I would never."

Damon reflected on that conversation with a warm, wistful smile. If the gods had their way, it would be among the last of the conversations Damon had with Darius on this side of his life.

The gods would not have their way.

The sun was nearly completely set in the mortal world, the last vestiges of daylight fading. That meant that the crowd should be appearing soon. At sunset, you see, the spirits of those who die descend into the Underworld. Once there, they are judged and sorted. The truly good and heroic people are taken into the fields of Elysium, where they can choose to remain or to shoot for the Isles of the Blessed. The fields of Asphodel await those who were neither particularly bad nor particularly good. The Fields of Punishment were for those who had committed special sins against man or against the divine. However, it was not spirits alone who came into the Underworld at sunset. Spirits do not know the way, and so they must have a guide. This guide is Hermes, the son of Zeus, most commonly known for being the messenger god and the god of travelers.

Most people would have to rely on Charon to ferry them back to the shores where the dead first arrive, but Damon had simply used a portal. So the son of Hades crouched, ignoring his stiff knees, and waited for Hermes to arrive.

5:29.

He took a deep yet quiet breath.

A bright flash of light illuminated the shores, and a cacophony of confused voices emerged. Damon's eyes caught a determined gleam. Finally. He listened to Charon yell over the voices, he heard the payment being made. Charon's boat had grown each year to accommodate the multitudes who died, but it always seemed to creak uneasily under the weight of all the souls.

Damon slowly, so slowly, lifted his eyes over the rock. Hermes stood in a white tunic with a gold belt wrapped around his waist. His caduceus, a staff with two snakes intertwined on it, was pointed towards the ground in his right hand. His helmet was tipped to the side, likely from wind rush.

"Gods, I hate this place. 'God of messengers and travelers,' they said. 'Help people with the biggest trip of all' they said. No specifics. You think maybe you're taking them to Artemis' temple in Ephesus, or to Disneyworld in Orlando, but no. It's the godforsaken Underworld," he heard the god grumble.

Time to move.

Damon leapt over the rock and ran at a full sprint toward the god, a blur of pale skin and dark clothes in the darkness of the world below.

Hermes sensed more than saw the boy, but even then he was too slow. Before he could turn around, Damon had kicked the god in the side of his knee. He delivered a strong left elbow into the god's mouth. Boxed the god's exposed ear. Hermes yelled in shock and whirled, swinging his caduceus in a wild haymaking attack. Damon ducked under the stuff and rolled into the god's legs to avoid the snapping snakes. The caduceus tumbled toward the Styx and Hermes toppled to the rocky ground. Damon grunted from the way the rocks had grated on him but rose swiftly nonetheless.

He had intended to seize the god and take him to the river bank, but the god's supernatural speed kicked into effect. Hermes was on his feet in a whirl, facing Damon in a boxing stance. It was too dark for the god to see what Damon was, but it was reasonable to assume he was no mortal. What living mortal waited in the Underworld to ambush a god? This lack of understanding spared Damon from being blasted into oblivion, but he still could not afford to be slow. He rushed once more, slipping a lead hook and landing a body shot in Hermes' stomach. The god stumbled backward, doubled slightly, and Damon sprang at the god with a jump kick. Hermes sidestepped, grabbed Damon by the crotch and by the leg, and threw him toward the Styx.

Damon landed with a loud grunt, and Hermes summoned his caduceus back into his hand.

"Who are you?" he demanded, striding confidently towards Damon.

The demigod was too breathless to answer, but not so breathless as to be unable to rise. He clambered to his feet with nothing but a rock in his hand. He suspected that Hermes still could not see him exactly but could distinguish how he moved. Still, he would not be expecting what he did next.

"Fine then. I can cause your essence to dissipate in the Styx without knowing who you are. Farewell, and may your final seconds be short," Hermes snarled.

He lunged with his caduceus with mind-boggling speed, but Damon had expected the lunge. In his hand the rock became a hand and a half sword, and as it did he pivoted away from the caduceus. He smacked the staff down toward the rocks and hopped closer to Hermes, sweeping his sword low and slicing the god's left hamstring. Hermes cried out in pain and Damon kicked the now kneeling god towards the Styx. Hermes tumbled until his head was right beside the river, and then Damon was sitting on his back, sword edge pressed to Hermes' throat.

"Who are you?" Hermes rasped once more.

Damon grinned, suddenly malevolent.

"I'm the one who will dissolve you in the Styx if you don't do as I say. Do you understand me?"

Hermes was silent for a moment, and then Damon could feel his back muscles tense.

"A demigod. Of course. So, tell me, son of the gods, are you my brother, my cousin, or my nephew? Please don't tell me you're my son," Hermes grunted.

"Cousin."

"Gods. You're Hades' boy, I wager. It all makes sense. The shadows concealed you so naturally. I thought you were some minor godling, but it would seem you are simply a foolish demigod."

"I didn't do all of this for a family reunion."

"No, of course not. So tell me, before I vaporize you, what would you like me to do?"

Damon rapped Hermes on the head and knocked the god's helmet to the shore. Instead of holding the god's head up, as he had been doing, he pushed it closer to the water. Hermes stifled a scream a second later.

"You know how miserable it'll feel to go into the depths, cousin. So, what I want you to do, unless you want to be dissolved, is swear on the Styx that you will do as I say."

Hermes moved to buck Damon, but once again Damon struck the god on the head, this time with his elbow. The sword in his hand took a small sip of blood from Hermes' throat. Hermes went slack swiftly.

"I swear on the Styx," he rasped.

"It's a simple request I have for you, Hermes. All I want is for you to bring me water from the River Mnemosyne. Bring it in a plain old plastic bottle that is perfectly intact. Bring it when I tell you to and bring it to me only. Nobody else can be told. Do I make myself clear?"

Hermes coughed deeply, prompting Damon to ease up on his blade.

"Fine, you wretched demigod. I'll do as you say. Now get off of me!"

Damon smirked and rose, stepping aside whole Hermes gagged and retched. He turned to face Damon and made a noise of disgust.

"Gods. You're just a kid. How did I ever let myself get this far gone?"

Damon maintained his smirk.

"You haven't fought since the days of Typhon? Maybe the Giants? Whereas I've been fighting every day for most of my life. You're stronger, but I'm better practiced. Don't take it personally."

Hermes glared for a moment.

"Be glad you're Hades' son. Otherwise, I'd vaporize you the moment my oath was up."

With that, Hermes vanished in a flash of light.

***

Once again, Adonis was kind enough to escort Damon back to Hades' palace. Damon had used a portal to go back to Elysium's gate, just in time for Adonis to arrive. Adonis was noticeably tense, and in a most unusual way, mostly kept his mouth shut. Damon did not care to look the gift horse in the mouth. He relished in the silence as Adonis walked back with him. Once again, as they neared the palace, *Hell's Bells* began to play on the bells. Adonis cursed fervently in Ancient Greek, which was a surprise. Adonis was not usually so crude.

"I'm just tired of the song!" Adonis snapped when he saw Damon's raised eyebrows.

An escort emerged from the ground, this time led by General Sherman of the Union Army. A battalion of Union soldiers with Henry repeater rifles filed around Adonis and Damon, marching uniformly down the corridor. Damon waited, anticipating a misfire or for a soldier to 'trip' and swing their rifle, but no such attack came. He almost asked Adonis what was wrong, but the stormy scowl on his face made him hesitate. As they neared the throne room, Damon heard Hades and Persephone's voices. It sounded as though they were in a heated banter. When the doors swung open, Hades was holding a vinyl album cover in his hand and pointing.

"You can't tell me these guys are not good! Look how cool they look!" Hades cried passionately.

Persephone threw her hands up in exasperation.

"All I'm saying, Lord of the Dead, is that there are other musicians and other bands. Remember how much you used to love Beethoven? Can't we go back to that phase for a little while?"

Hades sat back, crossed his arms, and glared defiantly.

"It's not a phase, Persephone. I'm a metal-head now, and there's nothing you can—" at that moment, Hades noticed the guard had brought in Adonis and Damon. A broad smile came to his face.

"Adonis! Donny!" he called, beaming.

"Zeus, grant me justice," Adonis groaned.

"How's that injury of yours, Adonis? I see you're walking better now," Hades asked, sympathy dripping like molasses from his voice.

Adonis cleared his throat.

"I'm fine, Lord Hades. Just ..." Adonis cast Persephone a bemused look, "a little bruised."

Hades nodded gravely.

"It's understandable. Go out and make sure you keep icing it. You wouldn't want that swelling to come back."

Adonis grimaced.

"No, lord. Farewell."

In a wisp of shadow and darkness, Adonis vanished from the room. This time, Persephone stayed behind. She regarded Damon with a rare interest that made Damon unsure of how he felt.

"Dad? Have I missed something?" Damon asked slowly.

Hades gave a slight smile.

"Oh ... Adonis was surprised when AC/DC blasted from my newly acquired stereo outside of his room, and it prompted him to fall off of his bed and land on his ... something. It was not a nice incident for him. But that's not important. What is important, and what I felt you should know, is that I have scheduled Darius' test for a week from now. On that day, Darius will prove whether or not he should be allowed a reincarnated state. I assume you'll want to be there."

Damon stared at his father, for a moment uncomprehending. *In a week? That would give Darius only a month's worth of preparation.* Damon could hardly imagine that would be enough. Darius was only eighteen! He could not be expected to do well on what was sure to be an incredibly grueling examination.

"Dad ... That can't be enough training time. There's no way."

Hades sat back on his throne. For the time being, he was a god and a king, not a father.

"I'm sorry you feel that way. Nevertheless, I'm afraid it cannot be rescheduled. If you are uncertain of training time, just remember that your Christmas break begins on Wednesday next week. You can spend the whole day on Wednesday and Thursday training with Darius."

"I don't want to overtrain him!" Damon protested.

"Then don't. Either way, the test is on Friday," Hades answered firmly.

"Hades, he's just a boy. There's no need to be that way," Persephone chided.

Hades shot her a look, but the look she shot back made him soften. He cleared his throat and wrung his hands, then shrank to a human height and approached Damon.

"I'm sorry, son. I have my obligations as a god, and I'm afraid I must meet them efficiently. That includes making sure Darius' test comes soon. Please understand me."

Damon stood for a moment, refusing to meet his father's face. *So soon? Darius could be gone so soon?* The idea was earth-shattering, but Damon eventually forced a weak smile.

"I understand."

Hades pulled Damon into a hug, and Damon was startled that he found the motion comforting.

"I know it's hard, son. But one day, you'll be reunited. I know it," Hades said softly.

Damon forced down the knot in his throat and stood more erect. Hades sighed and pulled away, throwing out his hand and shaping a portal back to Helena's apartment as he did so.

"Will I see you tomorrow?" Hades asked.

Damon shook his head numbly.

"I'm seeing Mara."

Hades nodded, then gave a soft smile.

"You've done well for yourself with her, Damon. I'm proud of you."

Damon walked towards the portal, at first unable to respond. Still, a wave of warmth filled him at his father's words, and he could not be silent as he left.

"Thanks for coming today, Dad."

Damon stepped through the portal, back into the mortal world. Hades stepped back as the portal closed, sighing heavily. He dismissed his soldiers and climbed back onto his throne. Beside him, after a moment, Persephone took his hand.

"You're doing the best you can," she assured him.

Hades nodded absently. The throne room was silent after that.

Things Go Awry

The knowledge that Darius' test was so close by made the days pass like cold syrup. He told Helena that he was worried Darius would do poorly because of how soon the test was. She knew, and really so did Damon, that this was not true. If Damon had thought that Darius would fail the exam, he actually would have felt better. If Darius failed, then that meant he would stay in Elysium. He would have his memories. Damon could still see his closest friend. But that was not his concern. Damon's fear came from a confidence that Darius could, in fact, pass his test. This fear nagged him for days on end. Helena tried to comfort him to the best of her ability, but the only light in this darkness was Mara. Her visit on Saturday had done much to bolster his spirit. The boy had not seen Mara laugh so much since the summer, and it did his heart good.

"Remember that time Kyle took up parkour and thought he was some sort of master after a couple of days?" Damon had asked at one point.

Mara cracked up at the memory she knew Damon alluded to.

"He was running down the street and tried to jump that bench and hit his shin on the back, and it made him flip over on his back. Oh my God, he was so messed up. Darius had to half carry him home."

That memory made Damon join in the laughter.

"His face! His face was priceless!"

That memory made him smile. They had parted agreeing to hang out again on Monday, though that had mostly been spent doing homework and complaining together. After that, it would be Saturday. In the meantime, Damon had work to do. He had a life to preserve.

"You jumped a god?" Darius exclaimed incredulously.

They were on the shores of the river in Elysium, alone once more. Damon hushed Darius with a hiss. He looked around in a panic, expecting to see any spirit eavesdropping. There were none that he could see and none that he could sense. He breathed a sigh of relief. More quietly, he went on with his explanation.

"Hermes was out of practice. That's all. Look, big picture, Darius. We have a chance to restore your memories even after you go into the Lethe. Hermes has sworn to bring me the bottle when he has it. We'll cheat the gods, bro! We'll make sure you never lose this life!"

Darius, however, did not seem to share Damon's enthusiasm. He sat back, contemplating the new information.

"Look, Damon, I'm not tryna sound … ungrateful, I guess. But if I get reincarnated into a whole new life, I'm gonna have new parents. Maybe a brother or sister. How is that gonna work, if in my head I'm still eighteen and my parents are actually Gregory and Donna? What if I'm reincarnated in England, and I remember my family and friends, but I never see them? I don't think I can live two lives like that, man."

Damon waved his hands around in frustration.

"Dude! I thought of this, didn't I? I already figured out a way around one rule. Why not another rule, or ten more? I can help you with all of that stuff. I helped get you to Elysium faster, and no one else could do that."

Darius closed his eyes, trying to think.

"You're a demigod, and you were able to pull strings for me once I was dead. But when I was alive, you helped me by being a human. You helped by being my friend. I'm not sure you can do as much as Hades' son up there."

Damon's jaw dropped in anger and in surprise.

"What is wrong with you, man? Do you want to lose your memories? Do you want to let go of all of this?"

Darius threw up his hands.

"I don't know! I just don't think I can have it both ways. Either I'm Darius, or I'm whoever the next guy is. But I didn't get to do enough good in my life before, and I want a second shot."

Damon opened his mouth to argue, then closed it again. He knew all of this. He had agreed to help Darius through this process. For Darius' sake, he stopped arguing.

"Fine. I'll keep helping you, and if you don't want the Mnemosyne water, I won't bring it to you."

The first part was true. The second part was the first lie Damon had told Darius since he had denied liking Mara back in freshman year. The two did not train after that conversation; they simply sat and talked. They skipped rocks, traded jokes, and recited Dave Chappelle lines back and forth. When Damon left, he was laughing. Still, his determination could not endure good humor for long. When he was away from Darius, he extended his hand and made a portal to take him to the banks of the Styx.

"Hermes, god of messengers, thieves, and travelers, to you I make my plea," he prayed, using a standard issue type of prayer to get the god's attention.

"Oh crap. Hades' kid, right?" came the grumbling response.

"You bet. I want that bottle. Now. Meet me at the Styx, the same spot from before."

Damon had anticipated a wait, or at least a portal to open to allow the god in. Instead, a blinding flash of light burst into his vision, and Hermes stepped out of it. His caduceus snakes hissed at Damon, and Hermes' expression was far from pleased. Nevertheless, he had not gone back on his oath. The bottle, a regular, generic, plastic thing, was filled with a water that was so blue it looked as though it were dyed. Still, it was a clear blue, the sort you see in the Caribbean that lets you see thirty feet towards the ocean floor.

"You actually got it," Damon marveled.

"You don't swear an oath on the Styx and break the thing. Now hurry up and take the crap so I can be done with you. No Amazon delivery will ever make it to your house on time again after this."

Damon did not take his time. He lunged for the bottle and snatched it from the god's hand greedily. He stared at the water, trying to distinguish any supernatural characteristic in it. There was nothing that he could spot. He eyed Hermes warily.

"This is the real thing?"

"Oh, my gods, kid. Yes, pesky little demigod, 'it is the real thing?' I did not swear on the Styx to break my oath. You can—" but here Hermes was cut off.

At that moment, a rumbling shook the ground, and suddenly dozens of skeletal warriors arose like they once did for Cadmus. They surrounded Hermes, who swung his staff instinctively. In a flash, three skeletons dissolved into thin air, but more were rising.

"Demigod! This is your doing!" Hermes roared.

"No! I don't understand what is happening," Damon cried back, willing the skeletons to fall back.

They did not obey the son of Hades but instead pressed in on Hermes. Damon moved then, rushing the nearest skeleton and snapping its neck in that moment. One skeleton pressed toward Damon with a sword raised, but Damon picked up a rock that turned into a pistol. With a loud bang and a buck of Damon's fist, that skeleton fell with a hole in its head. Hermes vaporized more skeletons, cursing as he did.

"Get away from me, you wretched corpses!" he ordered.

"Fine then," a voice as deep as a canyon called, "face a being that still has breath."

Hermes and Damon each whirled to face a looming figure in armor as black as the night sky. He wore no helmet, allowing his hair to flow behind him. In his hand, an iron sword with a rounded top rested. Hermes sucked in a breath simultaneously with Damon.

"Nope. Screw this. I'm out," Hermes surrendered.

"Good. Get out of my realm, Hermes," Hades ordered sternly.

The messenger god did not need any repeated order. He vanished into the light as swiftly as he had arrived. The skeletal warriors descended back into the earth. Finally, it was just Hades and Damon standing across from one another. Hades' face was expressionless as he stared at his son.

"Give me the bottle, Damon," the god demanded.

Damon stood in absolute terror. He knew, of course, that Hades had fought before, but seeing him in his war regalia was something that made Hades seem much more like a divine threat. Still, he could not abandon his plan. He raised the pistol in his hand with expert speed and shot at Hades. Faster than even Damon's eyes could perceive, Hades flicked his blade to deflect the bullet. Immediately, or so it seemed, the bottle of the Mnemosyne water exploded in Damon's hand.

"NO!" Damon yelled.

Once again, Hades stood listlessly, staring at Damon. The look he gave, that icy and calculating look, turned Damon's blood into erupting lava. He turned the gun in his hand into a broadsword and charged Hades furiously. He swung the blade with experienced practice, but Hades swept his blade so that the rounded part caught Damon's sword and forced it to the ground. The tip sank between the rocks, and Hades kicked Damon's wrist. Damon grunted loudly and clutched at his wrist, stumbling as he did away from his sword. The sword changed back into a rock. Damon then collected shadows and darkness into a ball and launched them at his father, but Hades sliced through the darkness in one sweeping motion.

"WHY?" Damon shouted.

Hades gave no answer. He simply let his sword dangle by his side. Damon bellowed in rage and rushed Hades once more. He sprang into a scissor kick in the air, but Hades pivoted aside and swung the flat of his blade like a baseball bat. The flat hit Damon dead in the center of his spine, launching him face first into the rocks.

"What? Shall it be said that the God of the Dead has faced Titans and Giants, but could not stand against his half-mortal son?" Hades asked calmly.

Damon clutched desperately at a rock to turn it into a weapon, but the rock did not transform. Hades clicked his tongue.

"They'll listen to me before they will you."

Damon rolled onto his back and stared up at Hades. Despite all of this, the god's face was still devoid of all emotion.

"You ruined everything! Darius could have, he could ..." but Damon could not finish the sentence. He heard Darius once more in his mind. *'I can't have it both ways.'*

Finally, Hades sighed. His armor morphed back into the black suit Damon had seen at school, and his sword vanished into a cloud of darkness. He walked to Damon's side and offered the demigod a hand, then pulled Damon to his feet. He dusted Damon's shoulders off, the father once more instead of the god. After a moment of Damon's stunned silence, Hades spoke.

"I'm afraid, my son, that in letting you spend so much time in the land of the dead, I neglected to explain to you the land of death."

Damon stared at his father uncomprehend-ingly.

"What in God's name are you talking about? This is the land of death."

Hades smiled ruefully.

"No, Damon. The world of the living is the land of death. It's the world of love and loss. There, heroes are often tragic, and villains are often the rulers. Here, in the world of the dead, those who are lucky get reunited with those they love. Up above, in the world you so adeptly straddle with this world, you lose those whom you love."

"But not me. I'm a son of the Underworld," Damon protested.

Hades sighed again and shook his head.

"So many of life's rules are exempt to you, Damon, but being human? That is not. Yes, you have a privilege in that you get to see many once they die, but that is not a guarantee. You can't decide Darius' fate because you're my son. Sometimes, even you have to lose a friend."

Damon clenched his fist.

"You're my father. Don't you want to help me preserve a friendship?"

Hades laughed without humor.

"I want many things, Damon. But my fate was to rule the Underworld as its god, and that means there are duties I must see through. That includes making sure that the reincarna-tion process proceeds as intended. Sometimes your roles in life contradict each other, and you have to resolve that tension the best you can. Men do that every day, whether they realize it or not. You have done it for years. You are a son of the living realm and a son of the realm of the dead. You are two things, but you have also put one before the other at times. Otherwise, why would you be here trying to do something absolutely asinine instead of with Mara?"

Damon was silent. Hades gave him a small smile.

"Go home, son. Spend tomorrow with your mother, with your friends, with whoever. But don't come here. Be among the living. You're more needed by the people there. Come to Darius' test when it's time. I will fetch you personally."

Hades circled his hand and created a portal, this time into Damon's room instead of anywhere open. Damon walked numbly into the portal; behind him, Hades turned his back. The god walked to where the Mnemosyne water had spilled. Sighing, the god caused it all to swirl into a little waterspout, then cast it into the Styx. There was still much to do.

***

Damon sat in his room for a long time, unmoving. His books, his weapons—knives and training staves, as of course, any demigod requires—and all of his electronics remained untouched. He simply sat in silence. It was not that he felt anything; it was more that he had an absence of feeling. In his mind's eye, Darius' words, Hermes' disappearance, and his father's terrifying armor performed a tireless dance.

'Can't have it both ways.'
'The world of love and loss.'

Could Hades be right? Could Darius be right? Damon tried to think about what Darius had said in particular. Was it possible that he had, in trying to help a friend, completely missed what he needed? Helping Mara had come easily enough. Damon had trained for most of his life to be able to break the greatest warriors, let alone an idiot in high school. Helping a soul in the next world? That was more complicated. He shuddered when he recalled firing at his father. He had been so desperate, but why? Darius had already said he did not want his memory restored after the Lethe. As Damon contemplated all of this, the door to his room gently creaked open. Light from the living room flooded the dark room as Helena stepped in.

Damon hardly noticed her. He squinted in the light but did not acknowledge her. Helena cracked the door behind her, then went cautiously to Damon's bed. She stood for a moment beside it, and finally, her son shrugged. She sat down beside him, still silent. Damon's ambivalence began to morph into nervousness. He could hardly think straight with Helena sitting beside him so silently. Finally, as he was mustering the energy to speak, Helena broke the silence.

"Your dad told me what happened."

That thought was not the most expected thing, though it was not a total shock. He had never thought much of his parents having contact, but it made sense, considering that Hades had known to come to the school after the Justin incident.

"I don't want to talk about it," Damon murmured.

Helena nodded.

"I didn't think you would. Why do you think I've let you stew for the last hour instead of making dinner?"

"Has it been that long?" Damon asked tonelessly.

"It has."

Damon shrugged. Helena sighed.

"Damon, why did you try so hard? You forced a god to do your errand. You tried to fight your father for that errand. Why do all that if Darius didn't even want it?"

Damon looked at his mother for the first time, and when he did his eyes narrowed into slits.

"How did Hades find out Darius didn't want the water?"

"I don't know that he has. I assumed because I knew Darius. I can't imagine that the boy I knew would want to remember everything from this life if he was going into another. It would hold him back too much."

"You keep saying you knew him. He's still around, Mom. You know him."

"Damon. Darius is dead."

"I know that."

"No, Damon, listen to me," Helena urged, gripping Damon's shoulders and turning him towards her, "Darius is gone."

The words hit Damon like a sack of bricks, but he refused to back down.

"Not yet. He's not gone yet. He may never be," he argued.

Helena's eyes began to tear up.

"Damon. What else can you do? Tell me. What can be done, short of sabotaging Darius during his exam, that you have not already done?"

Damon was a smart kid; he knew, of course, that his mother was right. But he knew it in the sense that he knew there was a galaxy called the Andromeda galaxy. It was a fact that had no impact or relevance in his thought process. So still yet, he argued as only a teenager can.

"Darius could still fail the examination! Why does he need the Blessed Isles? He has Elysium. He has The Fields of Paradise. And who knows? He's only had a little time to prepare."

"If you really thought Darius was going to fail, then why force a god to do your bidding? Why fight your father?"

Damon opened his mouth to argue, yet found he could not. Helena gave him a sad smile.

"I don't want to be right, Damon. I really don't. I wish you could see Darius every day, I wish he was coming over tomorrow. I wish you didn't have to deal with this. Just like I wish

Greg and Donna didn't have to. Or Mara, or Kyle. God, like me. Darius was like family to me, too. But you have to square with the fact that Darius may be gone for you, too."

That sack of bricks hit Damon once more, this time in the solar plexus. His breath was gone, and his skin was cold. She was right. God, he hated it, but she was right.

"Why?" he whispered.

Helena sighed heavily.

"God only knows. That's out of my realm of expertise. Sometimes crap happens. Whether it's the Moirai, or God's providence, or life just saying 'screw you,' things happen that even a demigod can't control. All you can do is make your choice as to how to respond. Darius has chosen to try to do more good in the world, and that just proves how heroic his spirit is."

"Proves how stupid I was," Damon grunted, choking back that annoying boulder that had come into his throat too often these days.

Helena pulled Damon to her in a tight embrace, and the tears began to fall from Damon's eyes as though pressed out.

"No, Damon, it proves you were heroically misguided. You did the sort of things that only a demigod could do in order to help a friend. But even you can't beat Death, hon. You were never meant to."

Damon registered what she said, but could hardly process it. His tears came easily now, so easily he hated it, and Helena rubbed his back as she had when Damon would get sick as a boy. Darius was dead. Darius would be gone soon. The truth of those words and their reality pressed his chest in like a slow moving truck. *Gone. How could that ever happen?* Damon had no answer. All he had was tears, and so he spilled them onto his mother's shoulder, just as Mara had done on his only days ago.

Moments passed like cold molasses, slow and thick, but they passed nonetheless. Perhaps ten minutes later, his tears had dried, and that odious feeling in his throat began to subside. When Damon was silent once more, Helena gently pulled away and surveyed his face. She gave him an empathetic smile.

"How hungry are you?"

"Starving," Damon choked out.

"I'll get dinner started. I'll let you know when it's done?" the last part sounded much more like a question than a statement. Damon sniffed and shook his head. He knew better than to let this feeling marinate.

"No. I'll come out with you ... Watch T.V. or something."

Helena nodded, seemingly relieved. She got up and walked out into the living room, which connected to the small kitchen. Damon walked out with her, silent as the grave. He went to the couch and flopped down on it. As Helena began to cook, she turned her music on once again. *Operator*, by Jim Croce, began to play, and Helena's sweet voice sang a harmony.

Numb once more, Damon reflected on what was to come. Darius would likely pass his test. He would be reincarnated. He would be gone, living a fresh new life, and Damon would likely never see him again on this side of life. Still, Damon thought, it would be alright. He would recognize that Darius would get to be a hero again, and then again, and he would one day smile fondly at the memory of his friend. He would come to accept his fate.

Behind him, Jim's guitar ceased to play for a second, and Damon muttered the line simultaneously with Jim.

"But that's not the way it feels."

The Examination

On Friday at noon, Damon Powers walked side by side with Hades, Lord of the Underworld, and a crew of heroes into a shadowy replica of the Coliseum in Rome. The heroes Achilles, Antigone, and Orpheus, were chosen to be the judges of the trial, as was often customary. These three having been some of the ancient world's most prominent heroes, they often decided matters of heroic worthiness. Damon had known them all since he was a boy, but being in their presence for this particular occasion made his stomach do a pirouette.

The five made their way through a hallway as devoid of light as primordial chaos. Torches lit with a blazing shadow lined the walls, and Damon shuddered. Finally, a dim light met them at the end of the tunnel, and the five stepped out into a large balcony, where a throne of bone and precious stone awaited. Hades strode regally to his throne and took a seat. Around the throne, four smaller chairs of regular wood appeared. Damon sat at his father's right hand, wringing his hands as he did. Beside him, Hades was devoid of expression. Behind him, the heroes leaned forward, intrigued.

Below, two soldiers stood at a gate. One was a Roman centurion; the other was a Napoleonic general. Silence echoed throughout the arena. After a moment of surveying the scene, Hades stood stiffly.

"Open the gate," he intoned.

The guards nodded, then stepped aside and raised their hands. The gate door, a grated iron material, ascended above the ground. When it did, Darius stepped out. Damon's heart sank upon seeing his friend, but not for the usual reasons. Most who would see their friends step into such a situation would be concerned for their safety. With Darius, the concern was that he looked too capable. He was shirtless, as was the custom, and his rippling V-taper made him look like a champion of old. His military boots crunched on the rough ground as he stepped out, and that sound followed the echo of the gate in haunting the arena. A moment passed, and that sound faded. Only then did Hades speak again.

"Begin."

Darius barely had time to react before the two guards charged him. One drew his gladius, and the other drew his pistol. Damon's heart seemed to stop beating as the Roman swiped at Darius' face. Darius ducked the swipe and punched the skeletal Roman in the jaw with a swift lead hook, then sprang away as the pistol fired.

Disarm, DISARM! Damon shouted mentally, suddenly afraid for his friend for the first time. As if hearing him, Darius seized hold of the Napoleonic soldier's elbow as he went for his rapier and kicked the soldier's knee. He ripped the sword free himself and decapitated the soldier with ease. With a weapon in hand, he turned to face the Roman. Their blades clashed and clacked, swept and swiped, but in the end, Damon was proven a good teacher. Darius took off the Roman's head next. The second skeleton collapsed, and the arena was quiet once more.

"Skillfully done, Darius," Hades remarked casually.

Darius looked at a loss for a moment before bowing his head in acknowledgment of the praise. Hades gave a grim smile and waved his hand; in a swirl of shadow, the sword in Darius' hand disappeared, along with the guards. Across the arena from Darius, a gunman stood with his gun aimed at a woman and her small child. Damon knew immediately what was about to happen and acted out of instinct, trying to summon a portal behind the gunman. The darkness would not move, and Hades quietly murmured, "It is not you I am testing, son."

Damon realized exactly what was intended, and tried to stand to shout a warning. A seatbelt, old and worn, suddenly wrapped around his waist and kept him in his chair. On the ground, Darius had already closed most of the distance between himself and the new arrivals. His old athleticism carried him in a dead-on sprint, and the gunman silently tensed. Darius saw the finger begin to squeeze, and as it did, he sprang into the air. Just as the gun began to buck in the man's fist, Darius was standing before the woman. The gunshot resounded, the child screamed, and Darius fell all in one moment.

"DARIUS!" Damon yelled.

"Quiet, Damon," Hades chided, as though he had spoken too loud in a library.

Hades waved his hand, and the new arrivals vanished just as the guards and the sword had. Darius was back on his feet then, free from any bullet wounds. He looked astonished, but Hades only said, "You're already dead. You can't die again."

Darius nodded, relieved, and Damon let out a breath he had not realized he was holding. Hades stared down for a long moment, analyzing Darius like a scientist watches his experiment take place. Darius met the look head-on, never averting his gaze.

"So far, young hero, you have performed well. Would you not agree, heroes?" Hades asked, turning to face the heroes. All in attendance nodded eagerly, impressed with what they had seen from a modern mortal.

Darius nodded in thanks.

"I had a good teacher," he replied.

Damon smiled ever so slightly. It was true; he had done well in training Darius. The boy had always been athletic, but his potential had truly been worked into acute skill. Hades broke a smile himself on hearing the praise.

"The first two tests are easy for most heroes. Courage to face a threat and the selflessness to sacrifice oneself comes naturally for them. It is the third which is always the hardest. I ask you, Darius, do you truly wish to proceed? It is not too late to back out."

Darius stood rooted for a long moment. His hesitation was understandable. Even above him, the three heroes were all shifting uncomfortably. They remembered too well the third trial, it seemed. Finally, Damon forced himself to make eye contact with his friend. He gave a nearly imperceptible nod. Darius took a deep breath and turned back to Hades.

"Bring on your trial."

Hades nodded, expecting the answer. Below Darius's sightline, he pat Damon's arm. Then Hades extended his hand across the arena. Out of the shadows, an imperialistic officer stood with imperial dignity. At waist level from the officer, a small boy with a shaved head knelt on both knees. His head was bowed, and his body quivered. A silver gun barrel was pressed into the top of his skull. Darius was moving swiftly then, attempting to parkour his way up the wall that hindered him from reaching the stands where the officer stood. Damon's blood turned to frost. Darius slipped on the wall and fell.

"NO! PLEASE, STOP!" Darius shouted; tears of panic filled his eyes.

The officer smiled silently. He cocked the pistol. The child whimpered. Damon tried everything in his imagination; he tried to summon a weapon, to teleport, to break from his seat. None of it worked. On the ground, Darius was searching frantically for a weapon. Seeing there was absolutely nothing, he whirled back to the stands. He leapt with all his might, trying to grab hold of the top and climb. His hand missed by two hands' breadth.

"PLEASE!" Darius screamed.

BOOM!

In a swirl of shadow, the Nazi disappeared. The child, meanwhile, toppled from the stands. He rolled underneath the rail and fell to the ground, landing at Darius' feet. Part of his head was gone. Damon threw up then. Darius stared in absolute horror. Then, slowly, a shadow danced by Darius' feet. The hero turned to regard it, but when he did, a pistol rested on the ground. It was a cocked revolver. Damon knew instinctively there was one bullet. The heroes sat motionless, completely fixated. Damon breathed heavily. His heart thundered as Darius lifted the revolver and regarded it in tears.

He lifted the gun to his head.

Hades was devoid of all emotion.

Then, with a loud, strangled cry, Darius whirled on Hades in rage even as the corpse of the child vanished in shadow. He pointed the gun up at Hades with a shaky hand.

"HOW DARE YOU?" he thundered at the god.

"How dare I what?" Hades asked innocently, leaning forward as he said it. Damon eyed his father in abject terror.

"You just let him kill that kid! You just sat there …" Darius trailed off, unable to speak through his fury.

Hades raised an eyebrow.

"Fate, mate. I had nothing to do with it. Couldn't. It's not my place. Instead, I gave you an out. Now, you're pointing that out at me."

"You call that an out? How could I kill myself knowing that something like that can happen? Who's going to make sure that nothing like it happens again?"

"You failed to do anything that time. What makes you think you can do anything to fight such a fate in the future?" Orpheus interjected.

Darius glowered over the barrel at Orpheus.

"It'll never happen again, if I can do anything about it," he snapped.

Hades stared at the gun for a long moment, and then his face broke into a broad smile. He snapped his fingers, and finally, the gun dissolved into shadow once more. The judges all nodded, and Damon's seat freed him to rise. Achilles spoke from his seat.

"Darius, you grasped the point of the test in its entirety. As a mortal, as a god, there are things you can't stop. There will be monsters you won't get to fight. There will be evils that gnaw at your conscience for ages to come, but they don't cripple you. They urge you to go out and fight what you can and put everything within your power to right. That is the spirit that heroes lose so often once they get comfortable in Elysium. It is a spirit, I see, that you have retained."

Darius stared uncomprehendingly at Hades.

"You're a monster."

Antigone gave a short laugh, speaking for the first time.

"Maybe, but Life can be the bigger monster. It throws things at you that you have no idea how to brave. Yet you somehow do it, even though you don't want to. You fight and dream of a better tomorrow. That's the essence of a hero. You passed that test just now."

Slowly, what she was saying began to take hold in Darius. His face lightened, and he eased up.

"I passed?"

"Indeed you did. So, now that all of that is over, there's nothing left to do but to wash. It is time to go to the Lethe."

So they went. Hades teleported Damon and Darius to the Lethe, right to the slight hill that rose above the bank of the river. Hades took Darius' shoulder and gave it a squeeze.

"It's a whole new life in that river, but that comes with letting go."

Darius nodded. Hades gave him a wistful smile, then cleared his throat. He cast Damon a furtive glance, then returned his attention to Darius.

"Darius. Allow me, just for a moment, to be a father again. You were one of Damon's closest friends in life. You took up for him, for Mara, for Kyle, and you gave something to each of their lives. You ... you didn't live long enough on this go around to become a father. But should you ever make it, you'll understand how grateful I am for that. My children ... they are often not welcome, in the land of the living. Thank you for being a good friend."

Darius's dark face colored a little more considerably. He coughed lightly, then answered the god.

"He was my friend too."

"He was. And so, as a parting gift from the God of the Dead, I will let you say your farewells. Damon," Hades addressed his son, "I'll ... Come find me in the palace when you're ready."

"You're leaving?" Damon asked, astonished.

Hades gave a slight smile.

"I think it's safe to say you're not going to do anything stupid."

With that, Hades vanished into the dark. Damon stared at his former place for a long moment before facing Darius. The two laughed awkwardly.

"So, um ... this is it," Damon said sheepishly.

"Yep. It is."

Silence. Neither could really say much or look at one another. Finally, Damon forced himself to look at his friend.

"You're my oldest friend, dude. You've been there for me every time I've ever needed it.

And I don't know how I am gonna make it without you. But ... If you're so set on making the world a better place," he said it with faked mockery, and Darius chuckled, "then I can't stop you."

Darius smiled and pulled Damon in for a bear hug. They pounded each other's backs, then pulled apart.

"It's been a crazy ride," Darius sighed.

"The best," Damon agreed.

Darius looked over his shoulder at the Lethe.

"We'll meet up again, right?" he asked, sounding nervous for the first time.

"God, yes. I don't know when, but soon enough, we'll meet up right here."

Darius nodded, then smiled. The two did a fist bump, just as they'd done for years. Darius then descended the bank and, mere inches from the bank, turned back.

"See you on the other side," he called.

"I'll be waiting," Damon smiled back.

Then Darius stepped into the river. He dropped fast, as though taken in by a rip current, but then resurfaced just as suddenly on the opposite bank. In a flash of light, Hermes appeared and grabbed the cleansed soul. He looked across the river and grunted when he saw Damon.

"Not jumping me again, are you?"

Damon shook his head silently. He found he could not speak, though no boulder was in his throat this time. Hermes eyed him warily, then softened.

"No hard feelings, kid," was all he said before he vanished with Darius.

That was all there was to it. The goodbyes were said. The trials, however horrific, had been brief. Darius was gone. Damon sat down on the bank, numb once more. Worse than Darius being dead, he was alive, and he was Darius no more. He meditated on that for some time.

When he took six hours to show up at the palace, Hades had been concerned that Damon had done something stupid. He teleported swiftly to the Lethe. There, he found his son asleep in the fetal position on the bank. Hades sighed deeply and knelt beside the boy. He scooped the demigod from the ground and straightened with a grunt. When he looked into his son's sleeping face, Hades felt a small pang.

"I'm sorry, son."

Damon said nothing. He was asleep, after all.

"I love you, Damon. I'm proud of you."

Damon slept on. Hades adjusted him so that he could hold him up with one arm, then called a portal. Moving gently, as to not wake Damon, he stepped into Damon's room and laid him on his bed. With a last look around his son's room, Hades stepped back into the Underworld.

Epilogue

Damon Powers sat with his back against the wall, reading about Orpheus trying to rescue Eurydice from the Underworld. Beside him, with her head resting on his shoulder, Mara played on her phone. Mara was doing a lot better. Since she and Damon had begun to date, two months prior to this, she had been worlds happier. She had begun writing poetry and was planning to study journalism, and was becoming quite good. Her arms were barren of fresh scars, and her mind was barren of a desire to cut. She had started this before she and Damon began dating, but their relationship was a dream come true for them both.

It had been three months since Darius was reincarnated, but of course, Damon and Helena alone knew that. Damon reached the point when Hades and Persephone agree to let Eurydice travel back before he shut the book and laid it on his bed. Mara looked up at him, putting her phone down.

"Are you alright?" she asked.

Damon rubbed his eyes wearily.

"Yeah, I'm fine. It's just ... Do you still miss Darius?"

Mara's gaze became a touch more wistful.

"Well, yeah. Of course, I do, but it's a lot easier now than ... well. Than before. Why? Are you having trouble?" she asked softly.

Damon shook his head as a no, and it was sincere. As a whole, he was fine. Still, the right story or the right memory could bring back that old numbness for a moment.

"No, it's just. Y'know. Sometimes, you just wish he was here."

"I get that."

Damon stared at his wall for a moment, then shook his head again and smiled slightly. He turned to Mara once more.

"I'm glad you're here," he said and meant it.

Mara smiled, but traces of concern were still on her face.

"I am too."

Damon breathed deep, contented with that. It had taken time to grieve Darius, but on the whole, he was content. He missed his friend every day, but he knew that somewhere, Darius was alive. He awaited that promised reunion with every memory, and always recalled what he had said before. *'In death, you're reunited.'* With that memory came words that he scarcely remembered, but could swear he'd heard before. *'I'm proud of you.'* Damon glanced at Mara once again, then looked around his room.

Life was pretty good too.

Spring Is So Annoying

Michelle M. Monagin

I hate spring.

It makes me nervous to see the snow start melting on the lawns. In January, when the daylight begins lasting longer than the dark, I start thinking of where to go this year so I can get away from the spring. In March, as the buds appear on the branches of trees, I realize it is time to go—time to run away from the spring. Then, even as I am running away, I'll be looking over my shoulder, watching for anyone following me—because I'm sure she's coming.

It wasn't always this way.

When I was a boy, I loved spring. When January came, I would begin watching the ice on the ponds and river to start breaking up. I often supplemented our diet with fish or crawfish during the spring months.

We lived outside the village, Mother and I. The only visitors we ever had were there on business—Mother was the resident Wise Woman. People would come from the village to buy charms from her. Charms to increase their crops. Charms to cure sickness. Charms to make someone fall in love with them. Charms to get a male child. And then, of course, they would come to her when their child was ready to be born because she was also the village midwife.

No one ever came by just to visit, though.

The other children would often laugh at me and call me little witch and bastard, although only where the adults couldn't hear. None of them wanted to be on Mother's bad side. The children didn't seem to think about what would happen when I told Mother about what they were saying to me. The first time one of the children called me a bastard, I went crying home to Mother. I didn't know what it meant, just that it was a bad name. I must have been around six or seven.

Once she knew what I was so upset about, Mother sighed and sat down next to me, putting her arm around my shoulders. "It means that you don't have a father," she told me. "It is just a description of your birth."

"If it's just a description," I asked, sniffling. "Why do they taunt me with it?"

I was pretty sure it wasn't a nice description. I wasn't sure why, and I'd be very surprised if the other children knew why, but I knew it was meant to hurt me. That was why it did hurt, even though I didn't understand.

Beside this, I knew other children who didn't have a father. Joseph's father died in the last war we had in the province, Andrew's father in the one before that. And little Marion's mother had died just the past year. No one was calling any of them a bastard.

"You are right," Mother told me. "They call you that to hurt you because you never had a father. It is because I was not married when you were born, and none of their parents know who your father is." She sighed again. "I suppose one of them heard their parents talking about me. The wives are always accusing their husbands of being your father."

"Why don't you tell them who my father is, then?" I asked, my tears drying on my cheeks.

She smiled and kissed the top of my head. "Because it is none of their business." That's what she always said when I brought up my father. It was nobody's business.

The best thing about the spring, when I was growing up, was that I could get away from the other children. During the winter it was cold, most of the animals were hibernating, and no plants grew in the winter. I had to stay close to home during the winter, too, most of the time. And it was almost impossible to cover my tracks when they lead through the snow on the ground.

But in the spring, when the days grew longer, and the weather grew warmer, the plants and the animals both woke up. Then I could stay away from the other children, ranging far away from the village alone. I knew the land around the village better than anyone else, and I could always lose anyone who tried to follow me. It is much harder to see tracks when there was no snow on the ground. By the time I turned sixteen, I knew several different ways to travel to the other villages in the area.

When I turned seventeen, I started working for the innkeeper at a town several miles away from my home village. No one in my village would take me on as an apprentice—though whether this was because of my bastard birth or my mother's status as the wise woman, I wasn't sure. The inn was around halfway between Athens and Thebes, so there was a good bit of travel going through there.

He liked me, the innkeeper. His wife had died several years before, and he had only the one daughter. His daughter liked me, too. The innkeeper was grooming me to take over when he died. His daughter, Madeline, was grooming me to become her husband. I liked both ideas.

Mother died the spring of the fourth year after I started working at the inn.

I'd moved her to a small house outside of my new town the fall after I started working there, so she could still be near me. The people of the town liked both of us better than the villagers ever had. Mother started to make friends— rather than just business acquaintances—and she seemed to be happy for the first time.

I noticed that she was coughing when I went to visit on my day off—not all the time, but sometimes she'd start, and she wouldn't be able to stop. It seemed to rob her of breath. I asked her if she was taking any of her remedies and she pointed to the table where there was a bottle of some syrup. That seemed to help, but I was worried. The problem was that she was the Wise Woman—I didn't know of anyone else who knew medicines better.

The next time I visited, she was in bed with a fever. Mostly it was a low-grade fever, and she was just listless. I could tell she didn't have the energy to talk to me, so I told her to close her eyes, and I tidied up the cottage for a while.

Then, when she woke up sometime later, she had bright red spots on her cheeks, and her eyes were strange. She didn't seem to recognize me, although I didn't realize that at first. She spoke to me as if she knew who I was, but she knew I was someone else besides her son. I thought she might be talking to my father, so I let it go on for a while.

She had never told me who my father was. I didn't know if he was alive or dead. I didn't know if he had known that she was pregnant when he left her. I didn't know anything about him, and I wanted to know.

She did give me a clue when she asked, "Does the lady know? Does she know that you come to me?"

I was so surprised that I asked, "What lady?" But that was a mistake. She seemed to come to herself, then, and realize who I was. She wouldn't say anything else about a lady or my father, even when she started talking again.

Then she started talking about sex, and I had to try to stop her.

Listening to your mother talk about sex is very alarming—at least to me. Who wants to hear his mother talk about sex? Mothers are not supposed to know about sex. Of course, I've heard girls express other opinions. They seem to have different relationships with their mothers—I suppose that would stand to reason.

I don't like to think of my mother having a sexual relationship with anyone, though. Maybe if she were married to my father, it would have been different—but I wouldn't want to hear about it, even then. It made me squirm when she talked to me as if I were the one that had the sexual relationship with her.

It was at that point that I went to hire a local woman to stay with her. I couldn't take that much time off to stay with her, even if I could have stood it. That was what I told myself, anyway. I wasn't running away; I had to work.

She died on the fourteenth of March. One of the village women was with her because I was working the dining room at the inn that night. She had seemed to be doing so much better that morning, and she had told me to go on and work my shift. So, I wasn't there when she died, and I didn't hear what she said. I only heard the message from the village woman when I got home that night.

"She said to be careful of the spring," the woman said to me.

"The spring?" I asked, blankly. There were no springs near the village. "What spring?"

"I don't know," the woman said, showing signs of impatience. She probably wanted to get home to her husband. "She didn't say which spring she was talking about. I'll be back in the morning with the other women to make her ready for her grave."

Then she left me alone with my mother's body. I sat next to Mother for a while, looking at her face. It was very serene, now. She didn't seem wasted or as if she had been sick at all. In fact, in the flickering firelight, she looked as if she was sleeping—as if she would wake at any moment and give me her warning first hand. But she didn't wake. After a while, I went to bed myself.

I forgot about my mother's dying message over the next few days—and about my father's lady. There was the business of arranging my mother's funeral, of course. I had to do all of that myself. Mother had died so unexpectedly that she hadn't had the chance to arrange anything. And then, the inn was busy because a number of parties were going back and forth between Athens and Thebes—some sort of diplomatic mission, I think.

By the time I had a chance to draw breath— three days after Mother's funeral, which was on March seventeenth—I had completely forgotten about the message she had left me. I was to be reminded of it soon.

On the twenty-first of March, two great trading parties came to the inn; one was going from Thebes to Athens, the second from Athens to Thebes. There was a great deal of confusion as they both arrived at once in our innyard with all their horses and baggage. And we had only two boys to take care of the horses, so the innkeeper, Madeline, and I all came out to help disentangle them.

And then there was one woman who walked in by herself.

I thought she was with one of the trading parties, at first. After all, she had appeared in the innyard at about the same time as the two parties arrived. Both parties had women as well as men, probably because they were trading so close to home and their women liked to shop in the other city. She was wearing clothes that were about the same as the other women—maybe a little bit better made, but I wouldn't know that. She didn't say she was not with either party. She didn't say anything at all at first.

I saw her first. She was standing alone off to the side, watching as women alit from the wagons and baggage was taken down. Her face was quite expressionless. She seemed to have a poor opinion of the operation. I tried to catch Madeline's attention, to point out this other lady, but she was helping a group of women already. So, I approached this lady as she stood off to the side, watching.

"Good afternoon, my Lady," I began, bowing to her from her side.

I was going to ask if I could help her in any way, but as my head came up from the bow, her head turned so that she was looking directly at me and her eyes caught me. There is no other way for me to explain what happened. Her eyes caught me, and I found myself unable to speak.

I wish I could say what color her eyes were. For all the times I looked into them. However,

I cannot remember. Sometimes I am sure they were the bright blue of a summer sky or the dark blue of the sea at dusk. Other times I think they were the green of the first leaves of spring. Still others they seem to be the rich, dark brown of good loam, freshly turned. That day, I would have said they were the bluish-white of the sky during a spring thunderstorm.

I just stood there as she inspected me and dismissed me. Then she turned her head back to the scene before the inn door. I felt myself swallow and I still could not speak.

"I wish to be served dinner," she told me as she watched the chaos before her. "I do not wish to wait."

I bowed again and said, "At once, my Lady." My voice was a bit squeaky, and I tried to clear my throat quietly. "Will you come this way?" That was better, I thought, gesturing toward the door of the inn.

The lady nodded her head and turned to walk as I had indicated. I followed her and opened the door when she reached it. She stopped just inside the door and looked around at the dining area. We were not busy at that time because it was after lunchtime and before dinner. Other than the two trading parties, there was no one at the inn. I pointed out a table near the fireplace where she might be comfortable, she went to it and sat down after giving me one more look.

After that, I sent Madeline in to wait on the lady, and I helped the traders unload their wagons. I didn't want to wait on her, although

I couldn't have said just why. She was as polite as any other guest that had come to the inn in the time I had worked there. Madeline gave me a look of disapproval, but she took over.

I went back outside, and I stayed there until both wagons were unloaded. Then I followed all our new guests into the dining room to start serving. It was some time before I could get Madeline alone to ask what she thought of the lady and if she knew which party the lady belonged to. In fact, it was not until both parties had settled down for the night. By that time, I had nearly forgotten the fright she had given me.

Madeline remembered, though. She cornered me after the last trader had gone to bed. "Do you know that lady?" she asked.

I thought she sounded suspicious, although I had never given her reason to be jealous. I started to worry, just a little bit. "No," I said. "Did she give you trouble? I thought she would respond better to a woman than to a man."

Madeline relaxed. "She made you nervous," she said with a smile. "So, you left her to me."

"She didn't give you any trouble, though, did she?" I asked this with concern. I didn't want to make it a habit of leaving difficult customers to Madeline. Honestly, I wasn't quite sure why she had made me so nervous.

"No, she was perfectly pleasant," Madeline told me, picking up her tray full of dirty dishes. "I just wondered because she was asking about your mother."

"My mother?" I asked her, blankly, opening the kitchen door and following her in.

"I assume so," Madeline said. "She asked about a woman who died a little less than a week ago. No one else has died in our village, have they?"

I made an agreeable noise and filled one of the basins with soapy water. I remembered my mother's words about a lady when she thought I was my father. Was this the lady? I washed the dishes and set them in the other basin that had clear water for rinsing. Madeline worked along with me for few minutes in silence, taking the dishes out of the clear water, drying them and stacking them on the counter.

When she spoke again, she sounded much more hesitant. "Do you think your mother knew her?"

I grimaced out the window, not wanting to look at Madeline. "No, I don't think so. I've never seen her before," I said. It wasn't a lie, I hadn't ever met this lady, and I wasn't sure she was the lady my mother had spoken about. "Did you notice her eyes?" I didn't wait for a reply. "I've never met anyone with eyes like hers. And I would think, if Mother had met her, she would have mentioned it." I washed a few more dishes, then I asked, "Did she ask anything else?"

"She asked about your mother's children," Madeline told me. She sounded a little bit nervous, now. "I told her that I was engaged to her only son. She wanted me to point you out."

I looked at her then. She was biting her lip like a little girl who knows she has done something wrong. I smiled and bent down to kiss her. "I'm sure it will be all right," I told her. I didn't think, at the time, that I was lying.

I went home that night—to Mother's house. I had been staying in one of the rooms at the inn since she had died, but now, with two large parties in residence for the night, there was no room for me. So, I slept at home in my cot beside the fire. It was an odd night. I usually don't dream—at least I don't remember my dreams—but that night I dreamt that my mother came to see me.

Mother shook me awake—in my dream—and smiled down at me as if she hadn't seen me for some time. In my dream, I was laying in my cot, and it was beside the fire. Everything was the same as when I had gone to bed, and I knew Mother was dead. But I wasn't alarmed, for some reason. It seemed perfectly natural that my dead mother would visit me.

"Hello, Mother," I murmured.

"You have to go," she told me.

Even that didn't alarm me at the time. I smiled up at her and said, "But it's night-time. Where would I go?"

"Go anywhere," she said. She was beginning to look—well, not alarmed, more annoyed. That seemed perfectly natural to me. She usually looked annoyed when she was talking to me. "You must leave here before morning."

"But why?" I asked, still not moving.

"I didn't know your father kept it a secret," she told me. "About you. I thought he'd told her years ago. Otherwise, I wouldn't have talked to her about you."

"Who is my father?" I asked. I asked it as if I hadn't been asking for years, and she hadn't been refusing to tell me. I asked as if I expected her to give me a name. And she did.

"Your father is Hades," she told me. "The problem is that he never told Persephone about you, and now she's angry."

I had closed my eyes at this time, and her voice was becoming fainter, though she sounded more upset the fainter she grew—or more exasperated, maybe. The last thing I heard her say was, "She's there, you have to run."

Then I fell into a deeper sleep, and I forgot about my dream. When I woke up, I felt there was something I ought to take care of, but I couldn't remember what it might be. I thought about it as I ate a crust of bread and washed. I still couldn't remember what I might have missed, but I thought it might have been something the innkeeper had asked me to do. I decided to hurry back to the inn and ask him.

I stepped out of my mother's house and turned around to close the door. When I turned back, the lady was standing in front of me. Then my dream came rushing back to me, and I wondered if it had been true. I was sure it was a real sending from my mother. I couldn't think of any other reason this lady would be visiting my home. However, I tried to smile and bow and keep my voice calm.

"How can I serve you this morning, Lady?" I asked.

She just looked at me for a moment, silent. She wasn't frowning or smiling. She didn't have any expression in her eyes at all. She just looked into my eyes. Finally, she spoke.

"You know who I am," she said. "Don't lie to me."

I hadn't quite opened my mouth, but I had thought about doing it, to deny the knowledge. I just stood there.

"You know who I am, and you know why I am here."

I swallowed before I opened my mouth. If she was Persephone, I could be in a lot of trouble, and I wanted to give myself a moment to think before I spoke. And, of course, if she wasn't Persephone, I didn't want to admit anything—I didn't know anything, after all.

"My lady," I said, carefully keeping my voice even. "I am not sure."

At my words, I saw the first expression I had seen come into her eyes. She looked annoyed. *Really,* I thought, *she reminds me of Mother.* Maybe Hades had a type.

"I am sure I have never seen you before," I told her. "I hope that I have done nothing to offend you, during your stay here."

"Who is your father?" she asked me. "What is his name?"

"My mother would never tell me," I said.

Her left eyebrow went up on her brow. "Never?" she asked. "What about last night?"

My mouth went dry at that. *She couldn't know what I had dreamt, could she?* I thought. Looking at her eyes, I felt that she could probably know anything she wanted to know. I tried to lick my lips with my dry tongue.

"My lady," I said, and my voice sounded very weak to my ears. "My mother is dead. She died six days ago. If I dreamt of her last night, I am sure it was only a dream."

I stepped back, then, because her eyes seemed to flash at me. Unfortunately, I had managed to lock the door before I had turned around and it stayed stubbornly closed.

She raised a hand as she stepped toward me and a flash of light blinded me. When I could see again, I seemed to be laying on the ground even though it felt as if I were still standing. I had to look up at her, and that felt strange—it felt as if I could turn my head farther than I had ever been able to turn it. I opened my mouth to say something—anything—but what came out was a caw, like a bird's cawing.

When I tried to move my arms to stand up, I realized that they were feathered. I turned my head almost all the way around so I could see myself and I found the body of a bird. A big bird, I was sure. I looked back at the lady and tried to ask what was going on, but all I could do was caw.

She knelt in front of me. She still looked annoyed, but not quite as angry as she had been. "You shouldn't have lied to me," she said, then she gave her hand a flick which threw me into the air.

I was terrified. I felt my wings open as I started to fall, but I was sure it wouldn't do any good. To my surprise, however, I glided forward rather than falling. I lowered one wing and felt myself turn. I flapped my wings and felt myself flying higher. I flew around mother's house once; then I landed on the roof where I hoped I would be out of her reach.

She was still standing there, looking up at me. "Next time," she said. "Don't lie to me." Then she turned around and walked away. It was almost a promise.

Since then it makes me nervous when I notice the days growing longer, or the snow melting on the ground. When the buds appear on the branches, I start thinking about moving farther north.

I hate spring.

The Best Laid Plans

Christina Lengyel

Hades had a son, the patsy, the pawn.
His mother made him in the dark but bore him in
the dawn.
In the sun he stayed,
Raised by the desert heat,
Longing for the cold,
A home he'd never meet.

Hades only 'raped' Persephone the one time, and even that time it was one of those situations where semantics were involved, and she really didn't feel comfortable calling it that. His reputation had already suffered a great deal due to the demands of his vocation, and, honestly, it was her mother Demeter's reaction—not her own—that everyone cared about anyway.

As it happened, by the time mother and daughter were reunited, Hades and Persephone had begun to get on quite well. In fact, they regularly and happily engaged in all manner of conjugal activity and had even taken to calling the situation above 'her royal temper tantrum.' It was ultimately pity for the cold and hungry victims of Demeter's grief that prompted the couple to arrange for the return of Persephone to the other gods, but her thoughtful husband issued her a pomegranate seed before she left so that she might return to their home for three months out of the year. Her mother, true to form, persisted in throwing elaborate fits during those months, but the humans became accustomed to it, and, knowing what to expect now, they were well-prepared.

So yes, strictly speaking, Persephone was technically kidnapped or 'raped' the first time, and she did not technically have control over the precise moment she'd return each subsequent time, but to her, the situation at it's very worst only ever amounted to an inconvenience, and that was usually after she'd had one too many glasses of wine and another fight with her husband about climate control in the antechamber of the throne room where she often stood in order to gaze out at the river of new arrivals to their kingdom.

Mostly, she enjoyed married life, and she spent the other nine months out of the year fairly listless as she waited to return to her home. Of course, she loved seeing her mother each spring and getting together with the other goddesses to run about sprinkling flowers and allergens all over the known world.

Often, she would sit with her good friend Ishtar and discuss the liminal nature of being. Occasionally, just for kicks, the two women would fill in for one another at minor feasts and ceremonies, but they showed the somber formality expected of them at the big ones. Persephone always attended with grace to the rites of the Eleusinian mysteries, delighting in the revelations of psychedelic farmers, no matter how repetitive they became. Her mother insisted they would be the most important rites the world would know, just as her grief for her daughter was the most important grief the world would know.

"Maybe," Persephone would say, but inside she would think about how everything has its age, and she would whisper in the nearest writer's ear some phrase, "a time to every purpose under heaven," or another.

It was by Persephone's own comings and goings that those gods, once outside of time, began to trace it. It might be noted that once time is traced, an ending begins to manifest, however nebulous, somewhere in the distance. So it was with Persephone's ascent that the descent of her kind was carved into the stone of destiny.

In fact, it would be Persephone herself who would give birth to that which would begin a new age in the world, an age where she would be a fairy tale at best and dangerous more often. As she made her trek in and out of the Underworld each year, she often contemplated what the next age would be like, if she'd be remembered and if she'd get to spend it with her husband. Would they be happy, the two of them together, alone, forever?

One of the sadder aspects of their marriage was that they could bear no children. For thousands of years, they made love. Persephone, a fertile and abundant goddess of spring was barren in her own home. The

Underworld is no place for conception. Birth and rebirth even may occur as a result of leaving that place, but it is only in the bright sunlight of the above that those acts are completed.

Hades, understanding of his wife's maternal desires, many times suggested she have children during the nine months she was away from him. She worried that if the timing was not perfect, she'd give birth in their home once she had returned, that the child would never be able to leave and live a proper life and that her husband would come to resent that child, a constant reminder of another man beside his wife. It simply wasn't worth the risk.

It was a sunny day in Spring when Ishtar hatched up a new plan. Persephone's light hair was becoming blonder in the sunlight, shedding the silver tone it tended to take on in her months at home. She wore a pink dress with a pomegranate red sash tied across her waist, and she sat upon a sit-upon stitched out of fine silk and filled with softest down. Ishtar in royal purple laid across a fainting couch, her volcanic black curls piled high onto her head and secured by a gold and diamond tiara. Between them was an elaborate spread on a large table. Hot tea, cold tea, wine, baklava, cheese, olives, bread, honeyed fruits, milk, cookies, lamb, boiled eggs, and a large hookah were at their disposal, though the two seemed relatively content and disinclined to partake in any of the offerings.

They were seated directly in the middle of a large field, one that would soon be filled with towering stalks of wheat, and were they not gods, it would have been a rather extraordinary sight. Being that they were gods, the farmer who had been in the middle of seeding that particular area, began immediately to offer his devotion and serve at table. He did so managing to choke down a few complaints that were swimming about in his throat given that this was the fifth year in a row the goddesses had chosen to have their lunch date in this particular location, and rather than being a boon, the event was a bit of a nuisance. The crowd that gathered a safe distance away to observe the affair interfered with his planting, and the whole thing set his schedule back by at least two days.

"I have an idea that absolutely has to work," cried Ishtar with the sort of overconfidence known well to gods and the wealthy. She waved her hand dismissively, and the farmer felt an auditory shift in his brain. They did this whenever they needed to be sure they had absolute privacy, and it left a ringing in his ears for several weeks following.

"Go on, my dear, but I can't imagine there's anything new under the sun. I've been thinking about this for literally thousands of years." She looked up at the sun and made a face, the kind of face you make at a relative who has gotten on your nerves.

"What if Hades comes here for you to conceive a child?" squeaked Ishtar, who seemed frankly too excited for an idea that almost certainly could not have been original.

"He can't. He has to stay in the Underworld."

"Well, what if someone with experience can watch it for him?" Ishtar puffed herself up high on her seat.

"He wouldn't leave without a good reason." Persephone sighed, the momentary hope that her friend might have had something clever to contribute having dissolved as quickly as it appeared.

"We can give him a good reason," said Ishtar, placing her hand on her hip and arching her back repeatedly and provocatively. The old farmer averted his eyes, his cheeks turning bright red. He reminded himself he had no right to take offense nor was it wise to take an interest when the gods acted saucily.

"Ishtar, I think you've been spending too much time here in the middle with the humans. Like them, you seem to overestimate the extent to which the God of the Underworld might be ruled by earthly desires." She rolled her eyes, picked up a fig from the table, examined it disinterestedly, and flicked it out of sight. Out of sight happened to be directly into the sight and right eye of the farmer, who very quietly doubled over and began to tend to his rapidly swelling eyelid, shaking his head furiously all the while.

"No, no, no, Poppy. It's not earthly desires but immortal love. If his wife is in danger, he'll surely come to her aid."

"What danger? What aid? 'Help, Your Highness! Your wife is trapped in a well, and only you can hump her out of it!'" She cast her forearm over her brow in mock helplessness before using one of the hookah tubes and a wine glass to replicate a lewd act.

The farmer, seeing this through one squinting eye, allowed his jaw to drop in horror and began considering how he would phrase a petition to Demeter to kindly not have the honor of hosting her daughter again.

"Well, not exactly. But you have to figure if he comes all the way up here to help you, what's another five minutes to celebrate your safety?"

"Only five minutes? That's no fun at all, Tara. But, let's say if for no other reason than to pass the time, we consider your plan. What sort of calamity would befit a goddess? What would possibly worry a god?"

"That is where our work lies, but I think our easiest route has to do with these humans. The ones that have taken to calling you Proserpina as of late have gotten ..." she paused for a moment to look all around her as if she might pull the appropriate phrase from the air, "so out of control," she concluded anticlimactically. "I have heard from more than one source that your neighbor to the East is so furious with the way they treat his devotees that he is ready to go like full deluge again."

"Oh, you know him. It'll be another thing tomorrow. Still, I agree that this is our best bet. These Romans seem to be possessing in abundance both power and folly. Let's talk somewhere else, though. I don't like the way this human is looking at us." The farmer was holding one hand over his eye and the other up to his ear, thinking perhaps the goddesses who seemed to have taken a sudden interest in him may have forgotten they had deafened him.

Ishtar waved her hand, restoring the man's hearing. "Here, sir," she shouted as one may do when they are trying to communicate with someone who does not speak the same language, even though she was speaking in perfect Greek. "We—" She gestured at herself and her friend. "are leaving now. You—" She pointed at him. "keep this stuff. Yum yum! You like!" She patted her tummy and smiled.

The farmer bowed as low as he could. "Many thanks, my Queens. You have so honored our people by your presence here," he mumbled.

"Oh, it's really no trouble at all," said Persephone as she straightened her sash and smoothed her dress. "May your harvest be plentiful."

With that, the two gods disappeared leaving the farmer looking desperately over at the crowd beginning to disperse a few hundred yards away. "Free food to anyone who helps me carry these things back to the village," he shouted. A few held up jugs of water and light baskets to indicate that their arms were otherwise occupied. Most simply walked away. A few small children ran up to the table, filling baskets with food which they began to eat immediately. There would only be scraps left by the time their short legs carried them all the way to town.

The farmer's two sons and a friend dutifully arrived to help carry the couch and table back to his house. This would be the third set he had to sell because he did not have room in his own house, and he could never sell them for what they were worth because no one in his village could afford furniture from the gods. A few women came and gathered the hookah, pillows, silks, and dishware. They all chatted blithely about the fashions and behaviors of the immortals as they resumed the real work of life.

Being both whimsical and immortal, the time it took Ishtar and Persephone to lay out their plan was relatively short. Three years was the blink of a god's eye, though it was also a large percentage of a farmer's life which was shortened significantly by the lasting effects of a herniated disk earned while carrying a particularly heavy metal throne back to his house after a luncheon in which Persephone was feeling 'extra royal.'

It should be noted that one day, toward the end of the farmer's life, the god Apollo heard about his sister Persephone's carelessness and fashioned wheels upon the metal throne, allowing the now paralytic old man to let the object of his suffering also be his chariot until the time of his death. It was his greatest disappointment, however, that after using his land for so many conversations, Persephone and Ishtar would enact their plans miles and miles away in the land of Judea.

It was in the twelfth month of the year that Ishtar and Persephone had completed their plan in which Ishtar arrived with great pomp and circumstance to Judea. She arrived as an apparition of her form, Esther, at the festival of Purim in a small but wealthy village. Here, she persuaded her audience that in order to overthrow the yoke of Roman oppression, they had to wait until the first days of spring in ten years' time. When the day came, they were to dress as Roman soldiers and capture the goddess they called Proserpina as she completed her ascent from the Underworld.

They would take the false goddess to the place of sacrifice, and there their god would lift her into the clouds where he would care for her and teach her the ways of the holy for ten years' time. In so doing, they would anger her mother, who the Romans called Ceres, who in her grief would cause the fields to fall fallow. The Jews, having long planned and stored for this occasion, would be well-prepared while the Roman soldiers slowly starved. Eventually, the Romans would be so desperate that they would seek the help of the Jews who seemed unscathed by the wrath of the gods.

The Jews would then pray to their god who reigned above all gods, prompting the return of Proserpina to Ceres and therefore the return of spring and the conversion of her followers to the Hebrew religion. So grateful would the Romans be that not only would the Jews be allowed to continue the business of living unmolested by persecution, but much like Mordecai who saved the Persian king from an untimely fate, their particular sect would be held in a place of highest honor by the Emperor.

The celebrants of Purim, having partaken freely of wine during the festival, were most grateful and overjoyed to receive this apparition. What they could not know because it was against their customs to follow the romances of false gods, was that another god, one arguably more powerful than Demeter, would unleash armies of the dead to retrieve his wife before he would let some unknown power hold her hostage for any time at all.

Ishtar and Persephone, on the other hand, were well aware that, like a child waving his father off to war till there was not a trace left of him on the horizon, the doting Hades would stand at the exit to the Underworld, following his wife with a loving gaze till his sister Demeter swept her away with the spring.

He would, therefore, see right away as the fake soldiers descended upon her, and he would no doubt step into the light to save her. Upon so doing, he would enchant the hearts of his sister Demeter and Persephone's beloved Ishtar who would be there waiting for the return of the goddess to the sunlight. The women would then easily persuade the ruler of the Underworld to remain with them for just an hour while Ishtar's most trusted twin sister made haste to watch over his kingdom. In this way, they might borrow a feast meant for the younger and elder goddess's reunion and dedicate it in Hades' own name in thanks and celebration of the enduring love which saved Persephone from foreign captivity.

It was during this feast that the married couple would consummate their love one last time before her return to their kingdom many months later. When Persephone returned to her kingdom and husband, she would be ready to deliver their child. The three would be a happy family, the child traveling freely above and below with Persephone. The plan, they thought, was flawless.

The ten years following Esther's appearance at Purim passed without much of note happening. Perhaps the most marvelous feat that occurred during that time was the fact that neither Ishtar nor Persephone uttered a word to anyone about their plan despite both being notorious gossips in the world of the immortals, each having ruined a handful of surprise parties in her day.

When it was finally time for the action to happen, everything went more or less as expected, the less being that Hades, a bit angrier than his wife had ever seen him, opened a crack in the earth which swallowed a dozen of the men who posed as soldiers that afternoon.

For this, Persephone later apologized to the god of the Jews while they made small talk at one of those incredibly dull meetings during which no one really knows why they were asked to attend, and between whispers about Hera's new hairstyle, promised him a sacrifice of her own to be delivered at some vague point in the future, reminding him that he owed a decade's surplus of food and supplies for his people in a hostile empire to her and Ishtar's plan. He conceded her point, accepted the promise of a future sacrifice, and extended his congratulations to her, as it was very clear by this point that her plan had been successful in the conception of a child, one she was expected to deliver the following month after her return to the Underworld, which would no doubt be the happiest of surprises to her dear husband.

Indeed, it was a surprise to her dear husband who stood with happy anticipation at the entrance to his kingdom while he waited for his wife to come make her descent.

"My darling!" he cried when he saw her round a bend and emerge into a clearing of trees. After gazing for a moment in astonishment, he corrected himself. "My darlings! How can this be?" He fell to his knees and outstretched his hands, never leaving the precipice of his realm.

"It's a miracle, my love! Well, it may have been methodical, but nevertheless, it's a miracle! We're having a baby." Holding her very swollen stomach, she ran as much as a pregnant woman can toward her husband. "I've missed you so," she cooed.

It was approximately one moment before their outstretched limbs would have touched that a rather imposing bolt of lightning came crashing down between them.

"Dad?" Persephone said, shielding her eyes and belly and looking upward.

"Brother?" Hades asked simultaneously.

"What in the name of all that is holy do you two think you are doing?" boomed a voice from the clouds, shortly before a god much shorter than one might expect appeared between the King and Queen of the Underworld.

"Well I was just on my way home, and Hades was here to meet me, and in three months I was going to head back up here and hang out with Mom. You know, the usual." While speaking, she adjusted her dress and posture a number of times, which made it seem like she thought if she sucked it in enough, she could belie the fact that she was nine months pregnant.

"I know what you're doing in general. I mean what are you doing with that?" He poked her stomach a bit more forcefully than is appropriate to touch a pregnant woman, and the child inside her kicked hard in response. "Lively one," he muttered, shaking the sting of the kick out of his hand.

"Well, I was thinking I might eat it. What do you think I'm doing, Father? I'm going to birth it and raise it and everything else, as one does."

"If I might interject, Brother Zeus, I feel like I can help clear things up by saying that this is literally the first I am hearing or seeing of any of this whatsoever." Hades crossed his hands behind his back and shifted his weight back and forth between his toes and heels.

"Oh, thank you, darling. How very helpful." Persephone gave her husband a withering stare, one that indicated it was going to be a very long and cold winter in the Underworld.

"Oh! Well, in that case! If this is the first you're hearing about it, then by all means, let me just rewrite the very Book of the Laws of the Universe to which I am also bound! No problem at all!" It was at this point that Zeus's voice began to reach a pitch so high that the nearby animals fled.

"What laws of the universe? What are you talking about?" Persephone asked.

"For the love of me, am I the only person in this whole family who picks up a book from time to time? Every other day one of you is whining, 'Why does he get to be in charge?' This. This is why I'm in charge. I'm the only one who pays any attention, basically ever."

"Right, well, that being said, Brother, I'm afraid I'm still not following your line of thinking," said Hades, now a slight tone of irritation in his voice. He, after all, was not only the oldest but the most levelheaded, which is, in fact, why he was the only one capable of spending eternity below deck without losing his mind and playing strange games with the soul of every mortal for all of eternity.

"My line of thinking, Brother, is that for one thing, no one, neither God nor mortal, can be born down there. Furthermore, it is generally frowned upon, Daughter, to go about making gods with neither the knowledge nor the consent of the other gods, especially the one fathering it!" His voice again reached a very high pitch.

Hades coughed. "I was there for the fathering bit, Brother. I just didn't know—didn't think it could—you know I have no children."

"Well, congratulations, Brother. Now you do. You have a son. One you'll never get to hold because he can never enter your realm. Very well done, Persephone. What a kindness. Honestly, you spend this long on a plan, and it never once occurs to you to consider the consequences."

"Fine, then. We'll build a house right here, and that will be that. It's the best we can do under the circumstances." Hades issued Persephone a glare more withering than hers had been, one only befitting the Lord of the Underworld.

"And what will you do during winter when both of you are down there? Throw the child scraps of human meat over the threshold?"

"My mother can come watch him. She'd be of far more use caring for her grandson than she is now, moping around for months on end."

"Good thinking! We should involve our darling sister in this discussion!" Zeus clapped his hands together enthusiastically. "Demeter? Demeter? Can you join us, please?"

Suddenly there appeared Persephone's mother, already with her kerchief in hand, prepared to weep and search for the next three months until her daughter's return.

"Oh, Poppy!" she cried at the sight of the girl.

"Oh, Poppy!" she shrieked, looking almost angry at her daughter's protruding belly. "What were you thinking?" She turned to the younger of her brothers. "You know no one in this family reads. It's right there in the Book of the Laws of the Universe. There's no having children down there." She wrung her hands despondently.

It was at precisely this moment that the god of the Hebrews arrived and stood quietly beside Zeus.

"What is this Book of the Laws of the Universe you people keep talking about?"

"Seriously?" interjected the newcomer. "It's like the only thing that has dominion over us, and you've never read the Book of the Laws of the Universe?" he asked unhelpfully.

"Right?" screeched Zeus.

"Yahweh," said Hades, nodding curtly at the god.

"Oh ... my ... me, what are you even doing here, Adonai?" squeaked Persephone before collapsing onto the ground. She clutched her stomach and began taking swift, deep breaths.

"I came for him," replied the god matter-of-factly. He pointed at her belly.

"Just wait one minute, now, friend. What right do you have to my son?" Hades demanded.

"Well for one, your wife promised me a sacrifice in exchange for my followers which you executed, if you will recall, while she carried out this ridiculous plan. I can't see why it matters to you anyway seeing as how the boy can never enter your realm."

"I'm sorry. She promised what?" screamed Hades, his voice the deep, loud bellow one might hope for from, say, a Thunder God.

While the men continued bickering about the fate of the coming child, Demeter calmly coached her daughter through childbirth. "One more push, love. You've got this."

"If this is true," seethed Hades, "and I have been but an unwitting pawn, then you, good Yahweh of the Hebrews, may have your sacrifice. May you have him, and may his shadow never cross the threshold of my kingdom. In all of his immortal days, I wish to meet him not!" With that, he spit at his wife and stormed down the long stone staircase that would return him to his throne.

"Well, I suppose that settles that," muttered Zeus, who had seen the outcomes of immortal games end with far more brutality than this one. His sister handed a squalling boy to him. "You, my grandson, you will be a god not of the Greeks but of the desert people. I wish you all the best." He kissed the boy's head and handed him over to Yahweh before disappearing back into the sky.

"Father? Mother?" Persephone cried, but she realized at that moment that she was suddenly all alone, and it was time for her to return to her husband's realm. In despair, she threw her body down the stone staircase, hoping that the fall might keep her from consciousness till spring came.

It did not.

***

Hades' son grew in the land of Judea, and he was called Judas. The god Yahweh cloaked him in the sentiment of a mortal so that he would not know of his heavenly parentage. Throughout his life, he searched for something he could never identify. He was led eventually to join a band of men and women who followed a man named Jesus they called the Christ, another god walking amongst the mortals. This Jesus hoped to help free the Jews from Roman oppression. The two were fast friends, and Jesus held Judas above all the other disciples. They spent a lot of time alone together, and it was during one of their evenings alone that Jesus asked Judas to do the unthinkable. "You and I are gods," he said, "and you'll be the one to prove it. Betray me, and we'll both be free."

"That's all well and good for you," said Judas. "But I'm no god."

"Of course you are. Let me tell you a story." There beside the campfire, Jesus took out a pouch of thirty Roman coins and revealed the history of Judas's family to him. Images of his parents and grandparents were etched into the silver pieces, even one with a scene of his father first taking his mother from her home.

Judas was filled with a series of emotions he felt ill-equipped to define, not the least of which being anger. At this point, Jesus filled Judas in on all the finer points of his plan. Rome would make him a sacrifice to the god of Judea, after which neither god nor man could hold dominion over those who accepted their freedom.

Judas was yet so filled with rage from this revelation that the notion of his best friend's death did nothing to alarm him, nothing to deter him. He agreed happily. Rome and all its gods, the family who so easily abandoned him, they would fall and suffer by his hand.

After he fulfilled his half of the mission, he took the bag of silver coins the Christ had given him and threw it in a fallow field. He then hung himself from a barren fig tree, a symbolic gesture as he now knew of his own immortality. There he hung, eyes and tongue bulging, waiting for his mother or grand-mother to arrive and weep at his feet for the mistake they had made.

If they ever did, they did not make themselves known to him. The god Yahweh no longer had any use for him either. After months had passed, with him still dangling, he finally decided to cut himself down and resume his lonesome immortal life upon the earth.

While hanging, he'd had a lot of time to think. Much like his mother before him, he was often unable to consider the consequences of his actions till after he had made his choices. In this case, he was to be known for all history the world over as a traitor, the one who led the lamb to the slaughter, the murderer of the one true god. It would never be known that he himself shared that immortal birthright, nor would people understand that he was acting in accordance with Jesus's will.

Furthermore, while Christ did eventually usher in a new age, one in which the Roman gods no longer reigned in the hearts of the people, Rome itself continued to reign, often brutally over the people, and they would eventually twist and shape Christ's story into a tool to maintain their own dominance.

Judas spent the rest of eternity being reminded by the mortals around him of his family who abandoned him, his friend who was abandoned by his followers in nearly every sense but his name, and his own unsalvageable reputation.

He took up odd jobs. Occasionally he showed up places he thought his mother might be, thinking maybe he could hurt her or maybe she'd come running into his arms and beg him for forgiveness. He was there in Alexandria when the library burned, and Hypatia was murdered. He did not find his mother. He often lingered near cliffs and crags in Greece, hoping to catch sight of the threshold of his father's kingdom, thinking if he could catch his eye, he might sit and talk with him at the edge. He did not find it.

The only god he ever saw was his grandfather. He would stand out in desert storms at night, the tallest thing around, lit up over and over by gorgeous forks of lightning.

Contributors

M. L. Allison

Ms. Allison is a Creative Writing under-graduate student at Washburn University and was part of the editing team responsible for this year's issue of Inscape.

Linda M. Crate

Linda M. Crate is a Pennsylvanian native born in Pittsburgh yet raised in the rural town of Conneautville. Her poetry, short stories, articles, and reviews have been published in a myriad of magazines both online and in print.

She has four published chapbooks: A Mermaid Crashing Into Dawn (Fowlpox Press - June 2013) Less Than A Man (The Camel Saloon - January 2014), If Tomorrow Never Comes (Scars Publications - August 2016), My Wings Were Made to Fly (Flutter Press, September 2017), and Splintered With Terror (Scars Publications, January 2018).

Noah Daniels

Noah Daniels is a third-year student at Wingate University. He is the student editor of the school magazine, Counterpoint.

Daniels lives in Monroe, North Carolina.

Christina Lengyel

Christina Lengyel is a writer of fiction and poetry. With a focus on language and consciousness, she has come to accept that often very little happens in her happenings.

She completed her MFA at the University of Baltimore and spends her time teaching college composition, practicing yoga, and hanging out with her husband, children, and friends.

Michelle M. Monagin

Michelle has been writing since she was fourteen years old. She writes primarily Science Fiction and Fantasy.

Michelle currently lives in Michigan and enjoys bike riding. You can follow her musings at:

www.michellemmonagin.com.

A Note from the Publisher

How to Thank a Contributor

Dear Reader,

Everyone at Zimbell House Publishing would like to thank you for reading the *Hades had a Son*. If you would like to thank a particular contributor, the best way is to leave a review for them. You may do so by leaving one on our Goodreads page, under the *Hades Had a Son* title, by using the link below:
http://www.goodreads.com/ZimbellHousePublishing
and be sure to mention the contributor directly.

Why leave a review? Reviews help budding authors build their credibility in the book industry. By posting a review on Goodreads, you help other readers find new authors they may wish to follow, and you never know, your review may end up on an author's website one day.

Friend us on Goodreads:
https://www.goodreads.com/ZimbellHousePublishing

Follow us on Twitter:
http://twitter.com/ZimbellHousePub

Other Anthologies from Zimbell House

The Fairy Tale Whisperer

The Mysteries of Suspense

Garden of the Goddesses

Elemental Foundations

Romantic Morsels

The Steam Chronicles

Pagan

Tales from the Grave

The Adventures of Pirates

Curse of the Tomb Seekers

Travelers

Dark Monsters

On a Dark and Snowy Night

Where Cowboys Roam

The Key

Veil of Secrets

Tournament Games

The Lost Door

Nocturnal Natures

It's an Urban Style of Love

The Neighbors

Date Night

Why? A Collection of Mysterious Tales

The Mountain Pass

River Tales

After Effect

Morsels from the Chef

Ghost Stories

Second Chance

Children of Zeus

A Nymph's Tale

Attack of the Federation

Coming Soon

from Zimbell House

Poseidon's Daughter

If I Say No

No Trace

Join our mailing list to receive updates on new releases, discounts, bonus content, and other great books from

Or visit us online to sign up at:

http://www.ZimbellHousePublishing.com

www.ingramcontent.com/pod-product-compliance
Lightning Source LLC
Chambersburg PA
CBHW051803050726
47598CB00006B/2409